W9-AHI-894

"I'm sorry, Jonah. I shouldn't have said all that."

He stood there, not knowing what to say. He hadn't expected Lovina's confession at all. Her words surprised him, especially since he loved Autumn, too. He hated to lose the baby when he'd grown so attached to her. Autumn could not stay with him and Lovina indefinitely—Jonah knew that. But it would break his heart once more when Bishop Yoder finally took the baby away.

"The bishop is trying to do what's best for Autumn," he said. "He won't give her to just anyone. She'll be loved by her new *familye*. Everything will work out fine."

Jonah didn't know why he bothered to reassure Lovina. Maybe he said the words out loud because he needed to hear them, too. But when she looked up at him, her eyes so wide and filled with doubt, he found himself suddenly longing to wrap his arms around her and kiss her tears away…

Leigh Bale is a *Publishers Weekly* bestselling author. She is the winner of the prestigious Golden Heart® Award and was a finalist for the Gayle Wilson Award of Excellence and the Booksellers' Best Award. The daughter of a retired US forest ranger, she holds a BA in history. Married in 1981 to the love of her life, Leigh and her professor husband have two children and two grandkids. You can reach her at leighbale.com.

Books by Leigh Bale

Love Inspired

Secret Amish Babies

The Midwife's Christmas Wish

Colorado Amish Courtships

Runaway Amish Bride
His Amish Choice
Her Amish Christmas Choice
Healing Their Amish Hearts
Her Amish Chaperone

Men of Wildfire

Her Firefighter Hero
Wildfire Sweethearts
Reunited by a Secret Child

Visit the Author Profile page at LoveInspired.com for more titles.

The Midwife's Christmas Wish

Leigh Bale

LOVE INSPIRED
INSPIRATIONAL ROMANCE

If you purchased this book without a cover you should be aware that this book is stolen property. It was reported as "unsold and destroyed" to the publisher, and neither the author nor the publisher has received any payment for this "stripped book."

LOVE INSPIRED®
INSPIRATIONAL ROMANCE

Recycling programs for this product may not exist in your area.

ISBN-13: 978-1-335-56736-9

The Midwife's Christmas Wish

Copyright © 2021 by Lora Lee Bale

All rights reserved. No part of this book may be used or reproduced in any manner whatsoever without written permission except in the case of brief quotations embodied in critical articles and reviews.

This is a work of fiction. Names, characters, places and incidents are either the product of the author's imagination or are used fictitiously. Any resemblance to actual persons, living or dead, businesses, companies, events or locales is entirely coincidental.

This edition published by arrangement with Harlequin Books S.A.

For questions and comments about the quality of this book, please contact us at CustomerService@Harlequin.com.

Love Inspired
22 Adelaide St. West, 40th Floor
Toronto, Ontario M5H 4E3, Canada
www.LoveInspired.com

Printed in U.S.A.

Why beholdest thou the mote that is in thy brother's eye, but considerest not the beam that is in thine own eye?… First cast out the beam out of thine own eye; and then shalt thou see clearly to cast out the mote out of thy brother's eye.

—*Matthew* 7:3, 7:5

Many thanks to Kim Woodard Osterholzer, who brings deeper meaning to safe and sacred home births. I appreciate your generosity, skill, insight and dedication to bringing God's children safely into the world. You, and other midwives like you, are amazing!

Chapter One

A white haze of clouds filled the bleak afternoon sky. Misting rain sprinkled the black asphalt of the parking lot. The late October weather had been mild...up until today. Stepping out onto the front steps of the small cinder block hospital in Riverton, Colorado, Lovina Albrecht wished she'd worn her rubber boots instead of her plain black shoes. Just now, her feet felt cold and damp. A chilly breeze rushed past and she shivered, catching the tangy aroma of damp earth and sage. No doubt the storm would increase and she was eager to get home before it struck.

Hunching her shoulders beneath the overhanging portico, she watched as an *Englisch* woman opened an umbrella and scurried toward her from the sidewalk. Lovina stepped aside to give the stranger room to pass and smiled before shyly ducking her head as the lady went inside. Lifting her face, Lovina breathed in deep, grateful for the rain. In this area, the farmers lived in a constant state of drought. They'd take any moisture they could get and consider it a blessing for their crops.

The intensity of the storm strengthened. Maybe Lovina should go back inside. But no. She'd rather wait here where she could be alone to think. Tucking an errant strand of golden hair beneath her black traveling bonnet, she readjusted the weight of her heavy bag on her arm and exhaled a sigh of relief. She'd accomplished her mission today: safely delivering Norma Albrecht and her unborn baby to where they could receive proper medical care.

As an Amish woman, Lovina had worked hard to become a certified professional midwife. Thankfully, her *Ordnung* was progressive enough to see the benefit of having a CPM in their community. Since legal authorities across the nation were prosecuting Amish midwives for practicing without a license, Lovina felt especially grateful. Even still, she only took on low-risk clients and was extra vigilant of them and their baby's needs. If any mother exhibited symptoms of distress, Lovina immediately referred them and their unborn child to the hospital in town. Which left Lovina no choice but to bring Norma here where one of the two medical doctors could help her.

The automatic double doors to the front entrance whooshed open and Jonah Lapp joined her. He looked like every other Amish man in the area with gray broadfall pants, black suspenders and scuffed work boots. Tufts of sand-colored hair peeked out from beneath the brim of his black felt hat. And yet Lovina could never consider him plain. Not with his long forehead, high cheekbones, blunt chin and deep brown eyes that always seemed to smolder with quiet intelligence. From what she'd observed over the past four years since he'd moved here, Jonah was a good man and dedicated to his elderly grandfather and Amish faith. His clean-shaven face attested that he was unmarried but that didn't matter to Lovina. She wasn't interested in him or any man. Not with the many skeletons she had clustered in her closet.

As Jonah tugged at the collar of his blue chambray shirt, he glanced out at the dismal day and quickly shrugged into his warm winter coat. "Brr, it's cold. Darrin just arrived and is with Norma. I think we can go *heemet* now."

Yes, she wanted to go home, too. He spoke in *Deitsch*, the German dialect their Amish people used among themselves.

"*Ja*, I saw him a few minutes ago. He can help make decisions for Norma and the *boppli*'s care. I'll check on Norma tomorrow," she said.

Stepping out into the rain, Lovina held the handrail as she negotiated the slick steps. The temperature had dropped and the wind picked up, slashing against her lavender skirts and spitting a fine mist of grit into her face.

Jonah followed. He worked part-time for the hospital as a certified EMT. Because they believed higher learning led to *Hochmut*, the pride of men, the Amish only went to school through the eighth grade. Like Lovina, Jonah felt fortunate to have his EMT credential, too.

"You don't have any errands to run in town, do you?" Jonah asked.

"*Ne*, I'm ready to go."

"*Gut*. If we leave for *heemet* now, we should be able to beat the storm before it gets worse," Jonah said.

Lovina hoped so. She hated the thought of being caught on the county road with a horse and buggy while rain slashed against their windshield. She didn't mind the inclement weather but it could diminish their visibility, and it wasn't safe with *Englisch* cars zipping past them like rockets.

Lovina and her *familye* had originated from Lancaster County, Pennsylvania, and had moved to Colorado when she was fifteen. They got lots of snow in Pennsylvania, but Colorado was colder, with a much shorter growing season. The farmers here depended on the moisture to produce their crops.

"I was hoping to repair the fence in the south pasture but doubt I'll get to it today." Jonah glanced up, blinking as droplets of rain spiked his long eyelashes.

In addition to being an EMT, he also owned the small farm where Lovina lived. She'd rented his farmhouse almost three months earlier. Because they both were single and didn't want the appearance of impropriety, Jonah lived with his grandfather out back in the *dawdi haus*, a small four-room house they'd built for his grandpa's use. A *dawdi haus* was the Amish version of a retirement home. Bishop Yoder, the leader of their congregation, had made the arrangements. Jonah needed the extra income from Lovina's rent and she needed a quiet place to live and serve her expectant mothers. Since Lovina's mom had died several years earlier, it was a vast improvement over renting a room from various members of her *Gmay*, her Amish community. Now that Lovina occupied Jonah's entire house, she'd set up a nursery and bedroom just for her clients. Her midwife business had flourished and she felt like she had a real home for the first time in years. But that could end the moment Jonah decided to marry. Yet he didn't seem eager to wed. Not since his broken engagement with Fannie Fisher eight months earlier.

"Do you think the storm will be a hard one?" Lovina ducked her head as they headed down the sidewalk.

"I hope so. We need the moisture," he said.

Without her asking, Jonah took hold of her elbow in a solicitous gesture meant to steady her on the slippery path. His fingers felt warm and firm through the fabric of her winter shawl but Lovina couldn't help feeling uncomfortable with his touch. He was a handsome man. There was no getting around it. And though she longed to encourage him, he was a cloying reminder of what she could never have: a husband and *familye* of her own.

The intensity of the storm increased and they hurried across the parking lot. Jonah's horse and buggy were tethered on the far side where the town had set up a covered hitching post just for the Amish to use.

"Do you know who that is?" Jonah asked, jutting his chin toward a parked car.

Lovina looked up, her gaze taking in a silver vehicle through the haze of the storm. A young *Englisch* woman of perhaps eighteen years stood out in the drizzling rain, leaning against the car's front fender. She wore blue jeans, navy tennis shoes and a yellow slicker. Her shoulder-length blond hair was damp and hung around her shoulders in sodden strands. At first sight of them, she braced away from the car and stared openly.

"*Ne*, I don't know her," Lovina spoke in a quiet voice.

Jonah glanced toward the *Englisch* girl and shook his head. "Me either."

"*Ach*, she seems highly interested in us." Lovina forced herself not to stare back as she skirted a puddle of water.

She couldn't help feeling a tad uncomfortable with the girl's gawking. But many people gaped at the Amish. Their distinct clothes and horses and buggies were an oddity that many *Englisch* people couldn't disregard.

"Maybe she's never seen an Amish person before," Jonah said.

"*Ja*, you're probably right." And yet Lovina sensed the girl's curiosity was something more. Something she didn't understand.

"Just ignore her," Jonah said.

Lovina looked away, focusing instead on her feet. With the temperature dropping so fast, the rain might freeze on the road and make travel more treacherous. It was definitely time to go home. And at that moment, Jonah's presence comforted her. He was a skilled horseman and knew how to drive in this kind of weather. But out of her peripheral vision, Lovina saw the *Englisch* woman tracking them closely, never taking her gaze off them.

When they reached the buggy, Jonah opened the door for her. As she lifted a hand to pull herself up inside, a loud revving of an engine caught her attention and she glanced back at the silver car. The *Englisch* girl had hopped into the vehicle, put it into gear and sped out of the parking lot. In the process, her reckless driving caused her to nearly hit a parked truck. She swerved in time to avoid a collision, her brakes squealing as her tires spat gravel. Both Jonah and Lovina stared as she pulled onto the main road and raced away.

"What on earth got into her?" Lovina asked.

Jonah shrugged his wide shoulders and wiped his damp face with a calloused hand. "Beats me. She seems awfully young. Maybe she hasn't had her driver's license long. She sure doesn't act like she knows what she's doing."

Chuckling at the eccentricities of the *Englisch*, Lovina nodded and climbed into the buggy. She immediately saw a large wicker basket sitting on the back seat, covered with several receiving blankets. While Jonah hurried around to climb into the driver's seat, Lovina stared at the object, wondering how it got there.

"What's wrong?" Jonah asked, taking the leather lead lines into his practiced grip and releasing the driving brake.

She nodded toward the basket. "What is that?"

He swiveled around and looked over his shoulder, his eyebrows crinkled in a confused frown. "Where did that come from?"

Without answering, Lovina jumped out of the buggy and looked up and down the street. Ignoring the thick drops of rain striking her face, she sought some sign of the silver car, but the vehicle was long gone. And all at once, a horrible feeling blanketed her. The realization that the *Englisch* girl had been watching them for a specific reason permeated her dazed mind. She wished she'd thought to get the license plate number on the car but she'd had no reason to do so. Now, she feared she'd regret it.

Turning, she climbed back inside. Ignoring Jonah's look of confusion, she closed the door tightly, shutting out the brisk wind. The quiet thud of raindrops striking the overhang seemed to escalate her nerves.

"*Ach*, dear me," she murmured beneath her breath.

"What is it? What's going on?" he asked, his eyes, forehead and mouth quirked in an endearing frown.

Shaking her head, Lovina reached into the back seat and pulled the basket close so she could inspect the contents. Just as she feared. Nestled within the folds of the warm blankets, a very tiny baby lay sleeping peacefully.

Jonah gasped in horror. "Where did that come from?"

"That is a girl," Lovina whispered, noticing the miniature dress the baby wore. It was handmade, the stitches even and tidy. Not at all like the factory-sewn jumpers so many of the *Englischers* put on their babies.

"*Ach*, you poor *liebchen*," Lovina crooned as she rested her fingers against the babe's arm.

The infant moved briefly, sticking a diminutive hand out, but she didn't awaken. Her small rosebud lips made a little sucking motion. The tiny nose, cheeks, chin, faint outline of eyebrows and fringe of eyelashes were absolutely perfect. Wonderfully formed and beautiful. And no matter how many new babies Lovina helped to enter this world, she could never get over the feeling she was witnessing the perfect miracle of life every single time. But more than that, this moment reminded her of a day twelve years earlier when she'd held her own precious newborn babe within her arms. Lovina had been only fourteen years old at the time. The father of her babe had been barely fifteen. Way too young to support a wife and child. Lovina had given birth to a lovely little boy but he was born out of wedlock to parents who were too young to raise him. Lovina was willing to try. She'd loved and adored her baby at first sight…until he was cruelly taken away from her without her permission and given to a childless Amish couple to raise as their own.

"Oh, *ne*!" Lovina murmured beneath her breath.

Her heart gave a powerful squeeze. She'd heard of this happening to other midwives but this was her first. A baby abandoned into her care. For Lovina, it was personal. Because she'd had a child out of wedlock, she could hardly stand the thought that somewhere in this world, there was a young mother who felt desperate enough to leave her child in the hands of complete strangers.

"Do you think the *Englisch* girl is her *mudder*?" Jonah asked.

"*Ja*, I most certainly do," Lovina said, wondering when the baby had eaten last. She searched the buggy but found no bottles or diapers. And since new babies must eat every two or three hours, she was filled with urgency.

"*Gucke!*" Jonah picked up a folded piece of paper tucked within the folds of the blanket and handed it to Lovina.

His deferential treatment didn't pass her notice. He was always solicitous and respectful of her. Always helpful. Yet there was a giant wall between them and she figured it was because everyone in their *Gmay* knew she'd given birth out of wedlock. To top it off, her father had left their Amish faith. He'd divorced her mom and married an *Englisch* woman and Lovina hadn't seen him since. Things like that weren't kept secret for long, especially since she'd lived in this community for years.

Some people tried to hide from their past. That wasn't possible for the Amish. When they relocated to another state, the bishops of the new and old community corresponded, to ensure the new person was still in good standing with their faith. Otherwise, they would be shunned. And more than anything, Lovina wished no one knew about her past. That she could be a normal young woman who went out with nice young men, married and had a *familye* of her own. But her history made it impossible. Because she was damaged goods. No Amish man would want her now.

Jonah watched Lovina carefully as she read the note. A myriad of emotions flashed across her pretty face. Her high forehead creased in a frown, her slightly upturned nose crinkled softly, and her full lips pursed in apprehension. Twining her finger around one of the black ribbons on her traveling bonnet, she gave a sad little gasp and her brilliant blue eyes widened before a flicker of dismay filled their depths.

"What does it say?" he asked.

She didn't answer for a moment, as if she was reading it a second time. Finally, she took a deep inhale and read out loud.

"'Dear Lovina Albrecht,

"'I've been told you are a midwife and are kind and generous. I can't be Amish anymore but I have no money to take care of my baby either. Her name is Autumn and she was born the second of this month. Her father is *Englisch* and wants nothing to do with us. I don't even know where he is. I want my *boppli* to be raised Amish by loving parents. That's why I'm giving her to you. Please don't try to find me. Take my daughter and care for her as your own. When she is old enough, tell her it's because I love her that I gave her up. One day, I hope she'll understand. Her life would be ruined if she stayed with me. *Gott* bless.'"

Lovina lowered the paper to her lap and pressed her fingertips against her mouth. Her expressive eyes glistened with tears and Jonah understood her consternation only too well. If anyone understood this situation, it was him. Having been raised by his grandparents, he'd lived the sadness and confusion of growing up never knowing his own mother. In fact, he had no idea who his father was. Little Autumn's mom had abandoned her, just like Jonah's mother had abandoned him shortly after he was born.

"What should we do?" Lovina lifted her pensive gaze to his.

Her eyes were filled with grief and a part of him hated to see her sad. Sighing, he knew exactly what his *Englisch* employers inside the hospital would want him to do. He should hand the baby over to the administrator. Right now. But in his heart, he knew that wasn't going to happen. Because he was Amish and so was this baby. And the Amish never, ever involved the *Englisch* in their lives unless it was absolutely, critically unavoidable.

"Her *mamm* was Amish, though it appears she has left her faith," Jonah said. "Her clothing looked *Englisch*. From her note, it's obvious she knows about you, so I'm guessing she must be from one of the Amish districts in our region."

"*Ja*, I think you're right. Little Autumn is definitely Amish," Lovina confirmed as she reached up and gently caressed the delicate stitching on the sleeping baby's lavender dress. The child wiggled and blinked her eyes open. She briefly made eye contact and remained calm. She wore a sober expression that seemed so wise and understanding, as if she understood her predicament but knew they would take care of her.

"*Ach*, she's so beautiful," Lovina whispered, leaning forward to gaze into the child's dark blue eyes.

"*Ja*, and she deserves better from her *mamm* than this," Jonah said.

Lovina jerked at the anger in his tone and

he forced himself to calm down. Though he frequently assisted Lovina in childbirth throughout their *Gmay* and had seen his fair share of newborns, he thought Autumn was the prettiest baby of them all. Her button nose, cheeks and eyes were impeccably formed and his heart ached with sorrow to know she wasn't wanted by her own mom.

"How dare her *mudder* abandon her like this?" he muttered to himself.

Lovina lifted her head and stared at him with wide eyes. "We mustn't judge. We don't know what the circumstances are or what her *mamm* might be going through. She looked incredibly young. She may be destitute and have no way to provide for her child."

That might be true. But…

"What about her *familye*? Surely they would help her," he said.

Most Amish families were quite large, living near their grandparents, aunts, uncles, cousins and siblings. And if that failed, the members of their *Gmay* would always come to the rescue. Their Amish congregation consisted of more than regular church meetings and a shared faith in Christ. It was an entire community of support, no matter the need. The Amish stuck together and took care of their own.

Lovina gazed at the baby. "Maybe something else is amiss here. We won't know until we find the *mudder*."

He nodded, expecting nothing less than absolute compassion from Lovina. She was so good and kind. Always earnest and giving as she tended the expectant mothers in their *Gmay*. And she doted on their new babies. Like everyone else, he knew she'd given away her own child. Maybe she felt guilty for what she'd done and was trying to make amends. It didn't matter to him. The last thing he wanted was to get involved with another woman. Not after the way his ex-fiancée had fractured his heart when she'd dumped him to marry another man in their *Gmay*. He thought she'd loved him but she'd proven him wrong, just like his mother.

The intensity of the rain increased as he sat back and stared out the windshield. His mind raced in a melee of thoughts. Everyone in their community knew his mom had abandoned him shortly after his birth. It wasn't a secret. But the Amish cherished all children, even illegitimate ones. Usually.

Although Jonah's grandparents raised him, he'd never felt like he belonged. Every woman he'd ever loved or cared about had abandoned him for one reason or other. First, his mom had ditched him for an *Englisch* life because she couldn't cope with being an unwed mother. Then his fiancée had dumped him when she learned his small farm was barely making ends meet. She feared the financial insecurity too much and married another man in their congregation whose *familye* owned one of the most prosperous farms in the area. Even Jonah's grandma had died when he was only thirteen. All these women had ducked out whenever things got rough. Other than his grandma, he'd been left feeling like he couldn't depend on any woman to stick it out with him.

Though the tenets of his faith taught that his primary goal should be to wed and raise a *familye* of his own, that would never happen. Not for him. Once upon a time, he'd wanted to marry. He dearly longed to belong to someone who cared about him. Someone he could shower his love upon in return. Now all he wanted was to sell his farm and move back east. As soon as he found the time, he'd speak with a real estate agent in town. A distant cousin in Ohio had offered him and his grandfather room and board in exchange for labor on his farm. Seeing his ex-fiancée so happy with her new husband at church and other gatherings had become too difficult for him to bear. It constantly rubbed salt in his wounded heart. He couldn't stay here anymore and watch her live a happy life with another man. He just couldn't!

Jonah glanced at Lovina, focusing on the matter at hand. Right now, they had to take care of this baby.

He inhaled a deep, settling breath and let it go. "According to the Safe Haven Law in Colorado, a *mudder* may deliver her uninjured *boppli* to a firefighter at a fire station or to a staff member at a hospital, with no questions asked. But the child can be no more than seventy-two hours old."

In unison, they turned and looked closely at Autumn, studying her wee little face. Jonah brushed the babe's hand with his index finger, checking her reflexes. She quickly tightened her grip around his thumb, which looked enormous in comparison to hers.

"According to the *mudder*'s note, this baby was born on October 2, which would make her twenty days old," he said. "Notice her face doesn't appear swollen and her eyes are quite clear and focused. She's definitely older than three days. I'm certain of it."

"*Ja*, I agree," Lovina said. "Maybe her *mamm* doesn't know about the Safe Haven Law."

Jonah agreed. The only reason he and Lovina knew about the law was because of their training as EMT and midwife.

The strong patter of rain caused Jonah to glance out the window. It was really coming down now.

"We should take her *heemet*," he said.

"*Ja*, I'd like to get her out of this damp air. But what will we do with her?" Lovina asked.

He peered through the dreary haze at the hospital. "We can't hand her over. This child isn't *Englisch*. And no matter what, the authorities will prosecute her *mudder* for abandonment and confiscate the *boppli*."

Lovina gasped, then made a sad noise in the back of her throat. Jonah knew the option of turning Autumn in upset her. It upset him, too. In his heart, he thought prosecution was the least the young mother deserved for abandoning her child but he knew the bishop of their *Gmay* would never agree. Autumn was Amish and they must take care of her, no matter what. It would be unacceptable for them to hand this innocent child over to the *Englisch* and their worldly ways. For Jonah, it was tantamount to throwing away one of *Gott*'s children when she was completely innocent and vulnerable. Jonah could never do that. Not ever!

Lovina shook her head. "If we turn Autumn in, social services will give her to an *Englisch familye* to raise. They'd never give her back to the Amish, especially if they find the *mudder* and prosecute her for abandonment."

Hearing his own fears verbalized caused Jonah's heart to clench. No matter what Autumn's mother had done, this baby deserved to be raised by her own people. She must remain Amish.

"We can't turn our backs on her," Lovina said.

"I agree," he said. "The *boppli* might have grandparents who want her. We need to look into this matter further and see if we can find them."

"But if that were the case, wouldn't the *mudder* have left Autumn with her grandparents instead of bringing her to me?" Lovina asked.

Her quick intellect always impressed Jonah. She always seemed to think the same way he did. But the fact that she'd given away her own child, even if it was years earlier, stood like a giant wall between them. Why had she given up her baby? He wanted to ask but it was none of his business.

"That's true," he said, "but it's possible

there's a greater problem here that we don't know about."

The concession was difficult for him. He'd always believed it was a mother's duty to put her child's welfare first. He couldn't condone abandoning a baby like this. Nor could he conceive of any scenario that would force a mother to do so. He didn't understand at all.

"Can't we consult with Bishop Yoder for his advice?" Lovina asked.

As usual, they were both on the same track. Jonah wasn't surprised. Frequently in their medical work together, they agreed on what to do.

"*Ja*, I think that would be best. We'll consult Bishop Yoder first," he said.

After all, everyone within the *Gmay* respected their bishop. He'd been elected to his position by the members of their congregation because he was devout, kind and generous and had a wisdom that seemed to surpass other men. He was also nonjudgmental and forgiving, doing everything in his power to lead and help the members of their congregation work, live and worship in joy and happiness. Rather than being domineering or dictatorial, he wanted their individual success. As a man of *Gott*, he truly seemed to want only what was right and good for others.

"We'll consult the bishop," Jonah confirmed.

With those final words, he slapped the lead lines against the horse's back and the buggy jerked forward.

As they pulled out of the parking lot, the rain intensified. Great, heavy drops of water pounded the windshield and saturated the hard, dry earth. Inwardly, Jonah smiled, knowing his farm was getting a good drenching.

He drove carefully, conscious of the horse's reactions to the rushing wind. The poor animal ducked his head and trotted forward, seeming eager to get home. No doubt the warm, dry barn and bale of hay beckoned to him. But Jonah didn't want to end up in a ditch. Not with Lovina and a newborn in the buggy. They should get the child indoors where she could be dry and warm as fast as possible, but he wouldn't travel at a breakneck pace, either.

Within fifteen minutes, Jonah saw his farm from a distance. Located just a mile outside of town, it was a lovely place with a fine house, a barn, corrals and fallow fields that had burgeoned with hay only weeks earlier. Now the harvest was over and Jonah could focus on his winter chores. The big drawback was that his place only had thirty acres of land. Jonah really needed thirty more to grow enough hay to be self-sufficient and provide feed for his horses and cattle. When he'd first bought the place, he'd thought it would be simple to buy more land. Hah! That was easier said than done. None of the surrounding farmers were interested in selling to him. Financially, it had become a hardship and he feared he might lose his farm. Then Bishop Yoder had asked if he'd be willing to study to become an EMT. Under the tutelage of Eli Stoltzfus, a member of their *Gmay* who was a certified paramedic, Jonah had gotten his certification and a part-time job at the hospital.

Then, several months earlier, the bishop had asked if Lovina could rent Jonah's farmhouse for her midwifery business. By that time, Jonah was certified and could occasionally assist with her work. Everyone, including the *Englisch* hospital administrators, thought it was an ideal situation. Because the *Englisch* doctors didn't understand their Amish ways, Jonah and Lovina were able to provide inroads to help their people receive better medical care. Everyone was happy, except Jonah. He didn't want to work with Lovina. He didn't want to spend any more time with her than necessary. And he felt guilty for feeling that way because he knew *Gott* wanted him to love everyone, even a woman who would abandon her baby. But the only reason he'd agreed to rent out his house to her was because he needed the extra income.

Between his farm work, the rent Lovina paid and his part-time EMT job, Jonah was finally making ends meet. Now would be an ideal time for him to marry. But with his fiancée breaking off their engagement last winter, he wasn't interested in any other woman. He had no reason to stay and try to make his farm prosper. It'd be better to sell it off and move on, which he planned to do just as soon as he could. Hopefully, it would only take a few months to sell. Then he could start fresh somewhere else where his ex-fiancée's betrayal wouldn't hurt so much.

Focusing on the road, his mind returned to the present. The bishop's farm was eight miles outside of town. Much too far to drive a new baby there in the middle of a rainstorm. Jonah didn't want to put Autumn at risk. He would drop the baby and Lovina off at his place, then go and fetch the bishop. It was the right thing to do. Because no matter what hurts he carried inside, he'd do anything in his power to protect this baby from harm.

Chapter Two

Lovina pushed the heavy barn door closed until she heard the latch click. Turning, she picked up a shiny metal bucket filled with frothy white goat's milk and made her way across the barnyard. She skirted mud puddles in the expansive driveway. The rain had stopped and the late-afternoon sun had begun its descent in the western sky. Jonah and the bishop should be returning any moment and she still hadn't fed the baby.

Focusing on the path in front of her, she struggled not to slosh any of the precious milk on the ground. Evie, the oldest of her black-and-white Nigerian dwarf goats, was normally docile and let Lovina milk her without trouble. But today, the goat had been obstinate and the process had taken longer than usual. And right now, Lovina was desperate to get back inside to feed Autumn. She'd left the baby sleeping peacefully in a wooden cradle in the nursery, but the child could awaken at any moment.

Gravel crunched beneath Lovina's feet as she scurried toward the house. A crisp, tangy scent of rain filled the air and she took a deep, calming breath.

Glancing up, she came to an abrupt halt. Darkness gathered around the white-frame, bi-level farmhouse. Two horses and buggies were parked beside the spacious garden plot. Lovina recognized one of them as Jonah's. The other one belonged to Bishop Yoder. Oh, dear! The two men were already inside. She must have been in the barn longer than she thought.

Hurrying on her way, she hoped Autumn hadn't woken up from her nap. It had been almost three hours since they'd found the baby in the hospital parking lot. She must be ravenous by now.

Flinging the screen door open, Lovina stepped inside the kitchen. With the cool temperature and rainstorm, the room felt chilly. After wiping her shoes on the large rag rug just inside the back door, she hurried to set the milk bucket on the kitchen counter, then reached for more wood to stoke the fire. She hesitated, noticing that someone had laid pieces of extra firewood in the bucket on the floor. Jonah, no doubt. Though he didn't seem to like her, he frequently brought her firewood whenever she met with an expectant mother. It was as if he knew she was occupied in caring for someone else and needed help. His consideration impressed her and, for one flashing moment, she wished they could be friends. But there always seemed to be an edge of irritation between them. As if they were purposefully trying not to like each other. And she knew *Gott* wouldn't approve of that. The Lord had taught that she should love everyone as herself. But no matter how hard she tried, Lovina still felt Jonah's censure.

The low sounds of men's voices filtered in from the living room, but she heard no cries from Autumn. Realizing the dinner hour had come and gone, she forced herself to remain calm as she stoked the fire, then quickly opened the gas-powered fridge. She lifted out a pot of chicken noodle soup she'd made early that morning and placed it on the propane-powered stove. With a quick twist of her wrist, she switched the burner on low. The soup would simmer while she prepared a bottle for the baby. Then she could offer the men something to eat. Her stomach rumbled with the thought of food and she realized neither she nor Jonah had eaten all day. But first things first.

Anxious to process the goat's milk, she went to see the men. Bishop Yoder sat on the plain brown couch. Jonah stood in front of the wide picture window, his legs slightly spread, his booted feet braced beneath him. It was a purely masculine stance but she forced herself not to dwell on that. Instead, she saw he was rocking gently back and forth, which was a bit odd. Again, she tried not to notice his lean hips, wide shoulders and muscular arms. She told herself his rugged good looks were worldly things she didn't care about.

"Hallo!" she called, startling both men.

The bishop immediately came to his feet in one quick movement as Jonah swiveled around to face her. He cradled little Autumn close against his chest and, all at once, Lovina understood why he'd been rocking.

"I didn't know you were here. You must have made *gut* time in the storm," she said, forcing a smile.

Standing beside Jonah, she gazed at Autumn's face, finding the baby wide-awake and sucking frantically on her tiny fist.

"We did. When we arrived, Autumn was

lying in her cradle, screaming her head off. We didn't know where you were, so I changed her diaper, then picked her up," Jonah said.

Lovina stared. Jonah had changed Autumn's diaper? How surprising. After all, he'd never been married or raised a child of his own. But she tried not to bristle at the censure in his voice.

"*Ach*, I was out milking the goat so I have something to feed her. If you'll hold her a bit longer, I'll get the milk processed as quickly as I can," Lovina said.

He nodded, avoiding her eyes.

"Is there anything I can help with?" the bishop asked, his gray eyes creased in a genuine smile.

Since the bishop was a veteran husband and father of nine children, Lovina wasn't surprised by his kind offer.

"*Ne*, I can handle it. But *komm* into the kitchen and we can chat while I work." She turned toward the other room and headed that way, expecting them to follow. And they did.

The tantalizing aroma of her soup drew the two men over to the cook stove.

"Um, that smells *gut*," the bishop said, nodding at her bubbling soup.

She gave him a warm smile. "Are you hungry?"

"I am. Jonah arrived to get me just as we were sitting down to dinner."

Which meant Jonah must be ravenous, too. Her own stomach rumbled but Autumn's needs came first.

As if on cue, the baby gave an irritated squeak. It was a high, adorable sound that made Lovina smile. Once the little girl was a few months older, the noise would undoubtedly shoot right through them. But for now, the baby was so tiny and sweet that everything about her was cute.

"There, there, Itty-Bit. You'll have your bottle soon enough," Jonah soothed her.

Itty-Bit! Lovina hid a look of surprise. She would never have expected a solemn man like Jonah Lapp to use such a term of endearment for a tiny baby girl.

As he tucked the child into the crook of his arm, Autumn immediately quieted…for the time being. Knowing they didn't have much time before her impatient cries turned into an ear-splitting screech, Lovina hurried with her chore. Picking up a metal spoon, she prepared to process the milk.

"*Ach*, she's *allrecht* now you have her. You're *gut* with children, I see." Bishop Yoder beamed at Jonah.

Lovina dropped the spoon into the stainless

steel sink. The baby jerked at the loud clatter and began to cry in earnest. Jonah bounced her harder.

As she retrieved a clean spoon, Lovina glanced at Jonah and saw a bit of panic in his eyes. Obviously he liked to hold babies... when they weren't crying.

"I'm glad you made it through the rainstorm okay. Did it create much mud on the road leading to your farm?" Lovina turned toward the stove.

The bishop glanced out the window. The shadows of dusk were settling across the land. "*Ja*, it did. The storm seems to have let up for the time being but it could start raining again. I should get *heemet* soon."

"You're always welcome here, bishop." Lovina glanced at Jonah, hoping for his approval as she used a coffee filter to sieve the goat's milk into a shiny pan she'd set in the sink.

"Of course," Jonah said, his voice sounding a bit strained.

The bishop smiled and reached to rub Autumn's tiny arm. Though she'd stopped crying, the baby released several exasperated grunts.

"She sure seems to have taken to you.

You're a natural at holding a *boppli*," the bishop told Jonah.

A flush of pink suffused Jonah's face and he looked embarrassed. Lovina felt the same way and, for the life of her, she didn't know why. She worked with babies almost every day of her life. So did Jonah. Being members of an Amish community that was constantly producing little ones provided lots of opportunities for both of them to hold and admire babies, not to mention their medical training. So why did this moment in time make her feel so uncomfortable?

Reaching for another pan, she prepared a double boiler to heat the milk. The back door opened and a rush of damp air that smelled of sagebrush filtered over them as Jonah's grandpa, Noah, came inside. Seeming to know the baby might be getting cold, Jonah tucked the warm blanket tighter around her little body, which won Lovina's approval.

"*Ach*, here you all are," Noah boomed in a cheery voice. "I saw Lovina come into the house after milking the goats." He glanced at her. "I brought you a bucket of chilled water from the well house. I figured you'd need it to process the milk."

"*Danke!*" Lovina smiled, thankful for his offering. Little Autumn's impatience was growing by the minute and she didn't want to leave right now to fetch the cold water.

"Hallo, Dawdi," Jonah greeted his grandfather.

Dawdi Noah nodded at his grandson, then glanced at the bishop. "I put your horse in the barn with ours until you're ready to leave. To what do we owe this unexpected visit?"

The bishop smiled and jerked a thumb toward Autumn. "I came to see this little one."

"Ach, what a pretty *boppli." Dawdi* Noah gazed with adoration at Autumn, seeking to make eye contact with the little girl. The baby gazed at him for several moments with somber tolerance. Then she waved her little arms and let out an outraged squall.

"Is she hungry?" *Dawdi* Noah asked.

"Ja! We're trying to get her fed," Jonah exclaimed, glancing at Lovina.

Determined to remain unruffled, she proceeded with her work. After all, she was a midwife and knew better than to get upset and scurry around like a maniac. All that would do was confuse and upset the mothers and babies she cared for. Instead, she made each of her movements count as she quickly stirred the milk and reached for glass jars to store it in.

She wasn't surprised by *Dawdi* Noah's curiosity. If he saw someone come into the house that he knew, which was almost everyone who came to visit, he came inside the house to chat with them. Mothers and their babies were in and out of this house at all times on any given day. *Dawdi* always wanted to hug and admire every single one. With a full head of shocking white hair and a jovial face creased by age, the elderly man stooped slightly and walked with the aid of a cane. Otherwise, the mischievous twinkle in his eyes made him look much younger than his eighty-nine years.

"Whose *boppli* is she?" *Dawdi* asked.

"That's what we're about to discuss," the bishop replied.

Dawdi tilted his head in confusion. "What do you mean?"

"*Dawdi*, this is a unique situation. Please sit down and you'll soon learn what's going on," Jonah told him.

Giving a nod, *Dawdi* sat on one of the wooden chairs and remained quiet yet attentive. The baby's cries became heart-wrenching and Jonah shifted her in his arms once more but nothing he did eased her wails. She was out of patience.

"She needs something to eat. I still can't believe her *mudder* would abandon her like this," Jonah mumbled beneath his breath.

Dawdi's bushy eyebrows shot up at this but he kept silent, his intelligent eyes taking in every movement in the room.

Lovina frowned and responded a bit too forcefully. "As I said before, it's not for us to judge. The bottle is almost prepared. Give me just a few more moments."

When it was ready, Lovina placed the pan of hot milk into the bucket of chilled water *Dawdi* had brought in from the well house so it would cool down as fast as possible. That would help the milk retain its good flavor.

"Can I hold her?" *Dawdi* reached to take Autumn from Jonah and he handed the child over.

Dawdi's hands were shaky and he almost dropped the little bundle. Just like catching a new calf in his arms, Jonah made a quick save as Lovina gasped.

"Careful!" Jonah said.

Dawdi nodded as Jonah placed Autumn in his grandfather's arms. Jonah hesitated a moment, as if waiting to ensure all was well before he withdrew the support of his hands. Autumn was so small and helpless, completely dependent upon them for her every need. And that made Lovina feel fiercely protective of the child. She'd do almost anything to keep this little girl safe.

The bishop sat at the table with *Dawdi* Noah and watched Lovina move efficiently around the room. This was her home and she knew her business, keeping a close eye on everyone as she worked. Jonah merely leaned against the wall and folded his arms.

"Has Jonah explained everything to you?" Lovina finally asked with a quick peek at the bishop.

Though he'd removed his black felt hat, the bishop still wore his coat and work boots. Otherwise, he was dressed just the same as Jonah and *Dawdi* Noah.

The bishop nodded. "*Ja*, he's told me how you found the *boppli* in your buggy in town and he let me read the note Autumn's *mudder* left her for you. I guess you weren't able to follow her."

Lovina laughed and lifted one hand in the air as she spoke in a teasing voice. "I'm afraid that would have been rather difficult."

The bishop chuckled. "Hmm, point taken. I know a horse and buggy could never catch a speeding car."

"Then you understand why we brought Autumn here instead of giving her to the hospital administrator," Lovina said. "We feared the *Englisch* would take her away for *gut*. Jonah thought it was for the best. So did I."

"I agree with your actions. From what Jonah has told me, Autumn's *mudder* would probably be prosecuted by the law for abandonment," the bishop said.

"That's correct." Lovina spoke as she worked. "If the *Englisch* took her, we might never get her back."

A dark frown deepened the furrows on the bishop's forehead. "That is unthinkable. Autumn is one of our *kinder*. She must be raised Amish. It's her birthright."

The bishop's words didn't surprise Lovina as she quickly prepared a five-ounce bottle, adding a mixture of powder especially for babies, which contained the proper ingredients to give Autumn enough calories, fat, protein and carbohydrates to keep her healthy.

As she reached for the tiny girl, Lovina almost tripped over Jonah's large feet. Without thinking, he shot out a hand to steady her. A feeling of shock and embarrassment prickled her skin where his strong fingers curled around her upper arm. She stared into his eyes, feeling transfixed for several moments. Then, she pulled away.

"I'm sorry," she murmured as he released her.

His startled expression told her he felt just as shocked as her.

"Um, if you don't need me anymore, I think I'll go outside and work on my chores," he said.

"That would be *allrecht*," the bishop said. "I'll speak with you again before I leave."

Jonah nodded and slipped out the back door. Watching him go, Lovina breathed a sigh of relief. She didn't know why she felt so jittery around him but she did. He'd made it clear what he thought about Autumn's mother and, because of her past, Lovina figured he must feel the same about her. And that realization set an ache in Lovina's heart that wouldn't go away.

In the barn, Jonah tossed grain to the chickens, then poured slop in the pig's trough. Normally, Lovina did the chores but she was occupied elsewhere.

It had grown dark, the sun hiding behind the western mountains. Not a single star gleamed in the night sky, and he figured they must be covered by rain clouds. The air felt damp and cold and he was eager to finish his chores and get something to eat. Right now, he was starving and thought about the delectable fragrance of Lovina's homemade chicken noodle soup. He dearly longed to eat a bowl or three but it was his habit to take his meals with *Dawdi* Noah in the *dawdi haus*.

Lovina was a good cook. Jonah couldn't deny it. He'd tasted her food at the church gatherings on numerous occasions. In fact, she was good at everything she did. When he'd been inside the farmhouse with the bishop, he couldn't help noticing how neat and tidy the rooms were now that she occupied the home. So different from the chaos that had reigned when he and *Dawdi* had lived there. By this time, Jonah had planned to be living there with Fannie, his ex-fiancée. Now he just wanted to leave town and go anywhere but here. And yet he sensed it was really his inner grief he longed to run away from.

His stomach rumbled again and he was eager to retire to the *dawdi haus* and whatever burnt dinner *Dawdi* planned to serve them tonight. Since it was so late, maybe they'd have a simple meal of store-bought bread, cold meat and cheese. And right now, that sounded like a feast.

He was just preparing to milk his two black-and-white Holsteins when *Dawdi* startled him out of his musings.

"Jonah, the bishop wants to see you again. Can you come up to the house?" the elderly man asked from the barn doors.

With a single nod, Jonah picked up the wood bucket and followed his grandfather. Wondering where the day had gone, Jonah walked through the dark farmyard toward the brightly lit house. His stomach churned with emptiness and he chafed at this delay. He didn't want to return to the house because he feared what the bishop might ask him to do.

Inside the farmhouse, he found Bishop Yoder sitting in the kitchen with Lovina. Steaming bowls of hot soup sat cooling on the table with a pile of warm biscuits and dishes of golden butter and honey. The baby was nowhere to be seen. Upon Jonah and *Dawdi*'s entry, Lovina stood and ladled two more bowls of soup for them. At first, Jonah just stared, his mouth salivating at the delicious aromas. Then he doffed his hat and sat down, too hungry to argue or refuse this kind offering.

When Lovina finally took a seat, the bishop smiled kindly. "I'm glad you're all here. Let us pray."

They each bowed their heads and prayed silently in their hearts. Jonah tried to focus on his Savior instead of the food sitting in front of him. Finally, the bishop released a low sigh and they each ate ravenously, the room silent except for the chink of spoons and knives against dishes.

After a few minutes, it occurred to Jonah that Lovina hadn't eaten today either. Yet she hadn't complained once. She'd merely ducked her head and done what she could for Autumn. And in that moment, Jonah couldn't help comparing her to Fannie. Though he'd been in love with his ex-fiancée, he realized she was naturally more high-strung… the complete opposite of Lovina. It was as if Fannie was uncertain of her own abilities and didn't know what to do. During their engagement, Jonah had thought she was young and fragile and needed a strong man to guide her. But now he wondered.

"It'll be *gut* for you to eat something hot before you take your journey *heemet*," Lovina said to the bishop.

"*Ja, danke* very much. It's delicious," the bishop replied, taking another bite.

As he reached for two warm biscuits, *Dawdi* smiled with delight. "*Ja, danke*, Lovina. This is *wundervoll.*"

She nodded and blessed the old man with a smile so bright Jonah had to blink. And for one insane moment, Jonah wondered what it would be like for her to smile that way at him.

When both *Dawdi* and the bishop glanced at Jonah, he took a quick gulp of chilled milk from his glass.

"Don't you think the food is *gut*, Jonah?" *Dawdi* asked.

Jonah didn't meet his grandfather's gaze as he swallowed hard and nodded, feeling embarrassed by his rudeness. "*Ja*, it's very tasty."

Lovina nodded but her smile didn't quite reach her eyes.

Avoiding her gaze, Jonah took another mouthful of soup, feeling grouchy because he didn't want to say thank you. In fact, he wished he was anywhere but here. But the food was absolutely yummy and he had no call to be discourteous. The Lord wouldn't approve.

"*Danke*, Lovina. It is very *gut*." He spoke without looking up, deciding it was right to speak the truth. He didn't want to like Lovina but the Lord would not endorse his ingratitude. Whether Jonah approved of this woman or not, she was one of *Gott*'s children and deserved his respect. He must not let his pride get the better of him. He should be humble and willing to help wherever he was needed.

"*Gaern gscheh*. You're welcome," she returned as she buttered a biscuit for herself.

"Where is the little one?" *Dawdi* asked.

"She went right to sleep after her bottle. Young *bopplin* sleep a lot, so I'm not concerned. She's only a few weeks old, after all. It's been a long, tiring day and she needs rest so she can grow strong," Lovina said.

"*Ach*, we have six Amish districts here in Colorado," the bishop said. "I'll send letters to each of their bishops to see if they know of any unwed *mudders* who might have run away. That way, we might be able to track down the *boppli*'s *mamm*."

Jonah chewed thoughtfully, then swallowed and set his spoon on the table. "That could take some time. If Autumn's *mudder* has run off, they might not know where she's gone."

"*Ja,*" Bishop Yoder agreed. "But if she's Amish, then she's one of our own. She may not have been baptized as a member of our faith yet, so she cannot be shunned for what she's done. We don't want to lose her to the *Englisch* world, if we can prevent it. I'm hoping we can find her and bring her back."

"What would you like us to do in the meantime?" Lovina asked.

Jonah leaned forward, his ears pricked for the answer. He had a bad feeling about this. The situation had been foisted upon them and they must rise to the occasion, for Autumn's sake.

"If it's *allrecht* with you, I'd like Autumn to remain here in your care for the time being," the bishop said.

There was a long pause as this soaked into each of their minds.

"Of course. I can tend to all her needs. It's no trouble at all," Lovina agreed with enthusiasm.

"Not just you but Jonah, too," the bishop said, swiveling in his seat to look at Jonah. "Even at such a young age, a *kinder* needs two parents."

Jonah's mind scattered. What exactly was the bishop asking him to do?

Bishop Yoder dipped his head. "I'd like Jonah to assist Lovina in any way possible. We must put this *boppli*'s needs above our own. I don't want anything to happen to her while she's in our care. She deserves the best we can give her until we can locate her *familye*."

"Of course," Jonah agreed. But he still didn't understand. It only took one person to feed, bathe and diaper a baby. With chores and livestock to tend, Jonah wouldn't be much help with that.

"I want Jonah to protect Autumn and Lovina," the bishop continued. "We don't know what or who we're dealing with yet. It's possible Autumn's *vadder* could return and try to take the *boppli*. We don't know if the man is abusive or what his motives might be. And I don't want Lovina to get injured because she's in the way."

Aha! Jonah hadn't thought about this but he realized the bishop was right, though he couldn't say he was happy about it. He didn't mind helping tend to the baby, but being Lovina's protector was something else entirely. Of course, he didn't want Lovina to get hurt but helping her with Autumn would mean he had to spend even more time with her than he already did with her midwifery practice.

From Lovina's frown and pursed lips, Jonah figured she felt the same about him. And that's when he realized she didn't like him any more than he liked her. And for some crazy reason, that made him feel even worse.

"The bishops in the area might not know if a girl in their *Gmay* had a *boppli* out of wedlock," Lovina said. "It would be quite easy to hide a pregnancy behind loose clothing."

"True, but we have to try," Bishop Yoder said. "It will take time to hear back through the mail. In the meantime, please take care of Autumn as if she were your own child."

Lovina nodded and looked away but not before Jonah saw tears glistening in her eyes. And that confused him even more. Other than the obvious reasons, why did she care what happened to this baby? Autumn wasn't her child. Lovina had given away her own babe years earlier, so why the show of emotion now?

"Will you have any problems if members of our *Gmay* ask questions? They can be rather nosy," the bishop said.

Lovina smiled at that. They all knew it was difficult to keep anything going on within the *Gmay* a secret for long. And that could work in their favor as they tried to find Autumn's mother.

"*Ne*, we'll simply speak the truth," Jonah said. "We'll say Autumn's *mudder* has asked Lovina to look after the *boppli* for the time being. Since they all know Lovina is a midwife, I think they'll accept that without becoming too inquisitive."

"*Gut*. And you'll keep this quiet, too, won't you, Noah?" Bishop Yoder glanced at Jonah's grandfather.

Dawdi nodded, his expression one of integrity that none of them would ever question. He was old but he had lived a devout life and was wise and kind. His character was unimpeachable and they knew he could keep silent on something as important as this.

"Of course," *Dawdi* said. "It's vital that we protect this *boppli*. I won't say a word."

Satisfied by this, the bishop nodded. "And while I search for the *mudder*, I want Jonah to accompany Lovina whenever she leaves the farm with the *boppli*. We must ensure that both are safe at all times."

The man glanced at Jonah and completely missed Lovina's shocked expression. She tossed Jonah a withering look that could have melted wax. Jonah gazed at the bishop with suspicion. He'd heard the man periodically give assignments like this to other couples in their *Gmay*, hoping to get them together in marriage. Their Amish community was new and relatively small and the bishop was trying to help their *Gmay* grow, to ensure their success. In fact, the bishop had recently assigned Ben Yoder to accompany Caroline Schwartz after she'd been badly injured in a buggy accident. The two had not gotten along…at first. Now they were newlyweds. Was that what the bishop was doing now?

Trying to get Jonah and Lovina together? Because if so, it wouldn't work. Not for Jonah. All he wanted was a fresh start. But with the bishop's word on the matter, Jonah knew neither he nor Lovina could refuse. Jonah would obey, but that didn't mean he liked it.

"I'll look after them both to the best of my ability and do everything I can to protect them," Jonah promised.

It wouldn't be easy. Jonah had his part-time EMT job at the hospital and Lovina had to pay visits to her expectant moms throughout the week. They'd figure it out. Maybe they could stagger their schedules.

Slapping the palms of his hands against the tabletop, Bishop Yoder scraped back his chair and stood. "*Gut.* I'll leave it in your hands. Let's touch base again at church in a couple weeks. If you hear any news before then, just send me word."

Both Lovina and Jonah nodded as they accompanied Bishop Yoder to the back door.

"I'll walk out to the barn with you." Lifting his cane, *Dawdi* snatched up another biscuit, then stepped out into the frigid night air with the bishop.

Jonah watched the two men disappear from view, noticing how his grandfather limped heavily on his cane. He knew the two men would go to the barn and hitch up the bishop's horse and buggy.

He glanced at Lovina. The heat in the room had given her cheeks a pretty rose color. In the warm glow of the gas-powered light overhead, her profile looked beautiful. With an apron tied around her waist and a dish towel draped over her left shoulder, she seemed so domestic. For a fleeting moment, Jonah caught a vision of her as some Amish man's wife with a passel of kids, but he quickly blinked that away.

"Unless you want me for something else, I'll head back to the barn, too. I need to finish my chores before I turn in. I'll feed your goats while I'm out there," he said.

She met his gaze without flinching, her expression a tad severe. "*Ja, danke.* Autumn and I will be just fine here without you."

Ah, that hurt. It wasn't so much what she said but the harsh, final sound of her voice.

"*Gut nacht*, then." He placed his straw hat on his head, then ducked outside and followed the other men to the barn.

Within minutes, the bishop's buggy rattled down the graveled lane as he headed home and Jonah milked his cows by kerosene light. *Dawdi* soon joined him, offering to feed the three goats. They closed the double barn doors, preserving what warmth they could find in the expansive barn.

As he worked, Jonah gazed through the shadows and a feeling of anticipation warred with a cold, dark dread. He'd see Lovina again in the morning. She might need to pay a visit to some expectant mother or run errands in town. He would need to accompany her while keeping up with his work on the farm. How long this might go on, he couldn't say. And what if Bishop Yoder failed to locate Autumn's mother? What would happen to the baby then? How would Lovina cope if the child was taken away and turned in to the legal authorities? Jonah shouldn't care at all. But he did. And that's what confused him most of all.

Chapter Three

Lovina lifted Autumn out of the plastic tub she used to bathe small babies and wrapped the child in a soft, fluffy towel. Droplets of water dotted Lovina's hands as she laid the tiny girl on a soft pad set on the kitchen table to dry her off. The room was toasty warm as Autumn kicked her spindly legs and waved her arms, active and wide-awake.

Streams of sunlight blazed through the window in front of the sink. Outside in the barnyard, a rooster crowed and Lovina knew it was past time to gather eggs. It was barely six o'clock in the morning. Normally, Lovina was ready to hitch up her buggy and pay visits to her expectant mothers. But today, she was way behind schedule. No doubt the three feedings during the night had something to do with it. Lovina had slept late but she couldn't begrudge Autumn. The infant's cries were innocent pleas of hunger. And each time Lovina prepared a bottle and rocked the baby, she was reminded that some other woman had gotten up in the middle of the night to tend to her newborn son years earlier and she viewed this service as a labor of love.

Once she had the baby dressed, Lovina lifted her up and cradled her in her arms. She spoke quietly to the babe, kissing her cheeks, telling her how wonderful she was. With her tummy full, Autumn gave a wide yawn and made little contented sounds in the back of her throat. Her eyes soon began to droop.

"*Ach*, are you tired already? Such a sleepy girl," Lovina cooed.

The baby looked at her briefly, her mouth curving in a reflexive smile. Though Autumn was too young to be smiling for real, Lovina's heart melted.

"*Ach*, you little sweetums. My dear *liebchen*."

A knock on the back door distracted her and she looked up. Jonah stood there, waiting for admittance.

Carrying the baby, Lovina walked over and opened the door. He held two pails of milk and, from the froth on top, she could tell one was cow's milk and the other was from her goats.

"*Guder mariye*! *Komm* in." Lovina stood back so he could enter the room.

He barely glanced her way as he set the pails on the kitchen counter. He wasn't wearing his felt hat and, from the damp tendrils of hair curling against his nape, she could tell he'd recently washed. He smelled of hay, horses and spearmint toothpaste...a masculine scent she'd been raised with and had always liked. It meant he'd been in the barn, working with his livestock.

"Since you're tied up with the *boppli*, I went ahead and fed and milked your goats. *Dawdi* is gathering the eggs for you now," he said.

How kind. For just a moment, a feeling of teamwork and *familye* washed over her. But then she reminded herself that this wasn't her *familye* and they never would be.

Jonah turned, his gaze sweeping the room. No doubt he saw the plastic tub she'd emptied and propped in the sink to drip dry and the bottle of baby lotion and thick towel she'd used on Autumn.

"*Danke*. That's very thoughtful of you," she said.

He looked at the baby and a half smile almost curved his full lips. Almost. His smile was so tentative she thought she must have imagined it. Regardless, she knew he liked the baby. A lot.

"Is she eating well?" he asked, lifting a finger to caress Autumn's tiny hand.

Lovina laughed. "Like a little piglet."

He nodded, his eyes sparkling with delight. But still, he didn't smile. "That's *gut*."

"Would you mind holding her a moment while I run upstairs?" Without permission, she placed Autumn in his arms.

A look of satisfaction curved his lips and Lovina knew he was pleased. As she turned toward the door, she wondered what it would take to get him to laugh.

Lifting Autumn to his shoulder, Jonah turned his face toward her little neck and inhaled deeply. "Mmm, she smells *gut*, just like a *boppli* should."

Lovina chuckled, pausing in the doorway. "Of course. She just had a bath and lotion. Most babies smell *gut*."

He cocked one eyebrow at her. "Unless they've spit up or, you know, messed their pants."

Lovina burst out laughing. She couldn't help it.

Jonah's cheeks flamed beet red, which made

her laugh even harder. But he turned away, obviously embarrassed by what he'd said.

"Don't worry. If Autumn messes her pants, I'll let you change her," she said.

From his profile, she saw him frown and she realized she shouldn't tease him. He seemed so surly all the time and she wished he would let down his guard and give her a genuine smile.

Leaving the two of them, Lovina hurried to one of the bedrooms upstairs, retrieved extra diapers and blankets, and was back in a flash. As she entered the kitchen, she heard Jonah speaking baby gibberish. He sat in one of the wooden chairs and had laid Autumn on his long thighs, rocking his legs back and forth and holding her tiny hands as he gazed down and spoke to her. The sight was so endearing that Lovina's heart gave a little squeeze.

With the baby occupied, Lovina reached for two frying pans, then opened the fridge to retrieve milk and a bowl of eggs.

"Have you and *Dawdi* eaten yet?" she asked as she cracked eggs into one pan.

Jonah responded without looking up. "*Ne*, not yet."

"*Gut*! I'll have breakfast ready in a jiffy. You did some of my chores, now I can repay you by feeding you."

He glanced up, a look of refusal on his face, but then he seemed to think better of it and glanced down. "*Danke*, I would appreciate that."

Lovina hid a satisfied smile. No doubt he was hungry and didn't want to pass on a good meal. But once more, that feeling of teamwork washed over her and she forced herself to shrug it off. She went about her work, processing the goat's milk as she had the night before, then prepared thick slices of homemade bread. She soon had oatmeal with raisins ready to round out their meal.

"Do you have a lot of work to do out in the fields today?" she asked as she worked.

He nodded. "*Ja*, there's a fence I need to repair before the cattle from the neighboring farm break through. We won't have rain today, so I thought I'd take advantage of the clear skies."

Holding a spatula aloft, she gazed at him. She hated to take him away from his work but there was something on her mind.

"I… I was wondering if I could buy two more goats," she finally said.

He looked up, lifting the baby to his shoulder. "You don't have enough already?"

She shook her head. He already knew she made goat cheese, which she sold to an *Eng-*

lisch grocery store in town every Friday. That left just enough milk to sell to some of the Amish mothers who wanted to supplement their baby's diets. Which meant there wasn't much left over for Autumn to eat.

"With the *boppli* requiring regular feedings, I fear I may run out of milk," she explained.

He nodded. "I see. We can't let that happen."

"*Ne*, of course not. I'm happy to pay you for the extra feed," she hurried on, fearing he might refuse her request.

He shrugged one powerful shoulder. "That won't be necessary. We can get you more goats if that's what you think we need. After all, it's for Autumn, and Bishop Yoder has asked us to care for her."

Yes, it was just an assignment from the bishop. That was all. Or was it? Somehow, teaming up with Jonah to care for this baby felt like so much more.

Lovina poured the fresh goat's milk into sterile jars and slid them into the fridge. She'd make cheese later this evening, once she had a few minutes for the chore. "I think it's best to buy two more goats but I have no idea how long Autumn will be here. If Bishop Yoder finds her *mudder* and she leaves in a few days, we could be stuck with two extra goats."

Glancing over her shoulder, she saw Jonah frown. Did the thought of extra goats bother him? Or did the baby leaving upset him as much as it did her? After all, Autumn's life was in flux and Lovina didn't want the child to return to a mother who didn't want her. Once Autumn left, Lovina knew she would worry about the little girl constantly. Memories of giving up her own child still clogged Lovina's chest, and she hated the thought of giving up another baby, even if Autumn didn't belong to her.

"I can drive you over to Mervin Schwartz's place this afternoon. He's got lots of extra goats. I'm sure he would sell us a couple of them. Would that be soon enough?" Jonah asked.

She nodded, feeling relieved by his offer. "*Ja*, that would be perfect."

Stepping over to the back door, she pushed the screen open and glanced around the expansive yard and outbuildings. It was warmer than the day before and the blue sky showed not a single cloud, which meant they would have no rain today.

"It's going to be a beautiful fall day. Where

is *Dawdi*? He should *komm* inside and eat," she said.

"He was in the coop last I saw him. Over the next few days, we're going to clean it out and add new mulch and a propane light for winter," Jonah said.

"*Gut*! I can help, if we do it when Autumn goes down for her nap." Stepping out onto the back porch, she let the screen door clap closed behind her as she cupped a hand around her mouth.

"*Dawdi* Noah," she yelled twice.

When there was no sign of him, she reached for the bell mounted on the side of the house and pulled on the leather cord. She clanged it several times, to get *Dawdi*'s attention. It rang loud and clear, the sound reaching clear out to the farthest field. On a farm like this, the bell was used only to call the *familye* in for meals or to herald an emergency. This was the first time Lovina had used it and she felt a little shy as she tugged the cord one last time.

Within moments, *Dawdi* appeared at the barn door, looking surprised and a bit alarmed.

"*Hallo! Mariye-esse,*" she announced breakfast.

He grinned and limped heavily on his

sturdy cane as he hurried toward the house with a basket of eggs.

Inside, Lovina took the eggs and served the men a delicious meal. They blessed the food, then explained to *Dawdi* their plan to buy more goats.

"That's *gut*. The *boppli* will need plenty to eat," he said, biting into a piece of bread spread with butter and strawberry jam.

"We'll be going over to the Schwartzes' farm later this afternoon. Do you want to *komm* with?" Lovina asked, thinking the ride wouldn't seem quite so somber with *Dawdi* along. The elder man had a penchant for chatter, the complete opposite of Jonah. Plus it might be fun for *Dawdi* to get away from the farm for a short time.

Dawdi stared at her a moment, as if thinking this over. Then he shook his head. "*Ne*, I have chores I need to do."

Like what? Perhaps he planned to start on the chicken coop today. But he offered no explanation as he tucked into his eggs and oatmeal. Lovina was mildly surprised he didn't offer to tend to the baby while they were gone. But maybe that was best. He was rather frail and shaky and she feared he might drop the child. Instead, she'd prepare a diaper bag, bundle the baby up nice and warm, and take her along.

Jonah didn't say a word, just ate his meal in silence. Occasionally, he glanced at Autumn and his face would soften for a few moments. Then he'd look at Lovina and the stern scowl reappeared.

Once he'd finished eating, *Dawdi* sat back and released a satisfied sigh as he rested a hand over the slight bulge of his stomach. A sudden frown drew his eyebrows together and he scooted back his chair.

"*Ach*, I'll leave you two alone now," he said. "I'm not feeling well all of a sudden. I think I have indigestion. The food was so *gut*, I fear I overate."

Jonah's mouth dropped open and he showed a look of concern. "Are you *allrecht*?"

"*Ja! Ja!* I just need to lie down a while," the old man said.

Lovina hid a smile. *Dawdi* had eaten enough for two men. But she got the feeling that he was trying to get her and Jonah alone. Lovina didn't mind taking Autumn with her. The weather was warm enough and Jonah would be there if she needed a second pair of hands.

Hmm. Funny how she'd already come to rely on the two men's help. But she wasn't sure she wanted it. Spending a good portion of the afternoon alone with Jonah might not be fun. His brooding looks could really send a chill through her at times. Hence, it might be a long, uncomfortable afternoon. For both of them.

Lovina held the baby in one arm. Using her free hand, she spread strawberry preserves on a slice of bread and spooned oatmeal into her own bowl. By the time she finished eating, Autumn was sound asleep.

Gulping down the last of his chilled milk, Jonah nodded at the infant. "Shall I put her in her cradle for you?"

Surprised by the offer, Lovina shook her head. "*Ne*, I can do it."

She stood, trying to hide her flaming cheeks and wondering what was wrong with her. He was only trying to help. But she didn't want him roaming around the back bedrooms of her home, even if it was his house she was renting. It felt much too personal.

"I'll be heading out to the fields now. I'll see you later this afternoon and we'll go get your goats," Jonah said.

"While we're out, I also need to check on Norma and her new baby. Just a quick follow-up," she said.

He nodded and she hurried to the nursery.

For some reason, she was suddenly desperate to get away from him.

When she heard the screen door close behind him, she breathed a sigh of relief. The bishop had asked the two of them to care for Autumn, but for some reason, this situation felt much too intimate for Lovina. With Jonah and his grandfather sitting in her kitchen, eating a meal she'd prepared, holding and marveling at the baby, it felt like they were a real *familye*. And they weren't. Not now, not ever. But it served Lovina right for inviting the men to share her meal. She'd tried to be friendly and helpful. After all, they'd milked her goats and gathered her eggs. But getting close to Jonah and his sweet grandfather was the last thing she wanted. Because their time together was temporary at best.

Jonah hurried out to the barn, where he gathered up his shovel and hammer and a bag of nails. Within minutes, he was headed out to the south pasture. As he stepped over furrows of damp, fertile soil, he gazed at the Wet Mountains where stands of aspen stood high up, shimmering in the sunshine. Thick stands of scrub oak trailed the fence line where his property bordered the fields of another *Englisch* farmer where the fields lay fallow. For two years now, no crops had grown there. Though Jonah had twice made an offer to buy the acreage, the elderly *Englisch* man who owned the land refused.

Shaking his head, Jonah pulled the brim of his felt hat lower to shade his eyes. Leaving good, fertile soil empty was such a waste. If Jonah owned the land, he'd fill it with hay or a little barley or oats.

Since he didn't have enough of his own land to plant, Jonah had to buy his barley and oats from another farmer. And though he knew it was wrong to covet what belonged to someone else, he admired the open fields surrounding his place. But then he thought better of it. Today or tomorrow, he'd speak to a real estate agent in town and hopefully sell his farm soon. At some point, he'd need to tell Lovina of his plans so she could find another place to live. He'd move back east where he could start anew. Maybe, in time, he'd even meet someone he could love. Someone who would love him in return. But right now, that seemed like a distant dream.

Adjusting the weight of the shovel in his hand, he thought about Lovina. She hadn't hesitated when the bishop asked her to care for Autumn. This morning, when she'd invited him and *Dawdi* to breakfast, he could see the fatigue in her eyes. No doubt, she'd been up throughout the night with the baby. And yet she hadn't grumbled about it. Not once. He couldn't help comparing her to Fannie, who'd exhibited great concern when he confided his farm wasn't making ends meet. Within a fortnight, she'd broken off their engagement. And though she hadn't said so, he knew she wanted more security than he could offer. His suspicions had been confirmed when she'd quickly become engaged to Alvin Fisher, whose father owned a lucrative farm.

Shaking his head, Jonah refocused his thoughts on his work. At the irrigation ditch, he studied the long rows where just weeks earlier he'd mowed his fall hay. He discovered several places where the rainwater had pooled and created a big sinkhole. He evened out the furrows and built up the side of the ditch so the winter moisture wouldn't cause more erosion.

As he worked, droplets of sweat formed on his brow in spite of the cool day. Standing up straight, he pushed back his hat and swiped his forehead with the sleeve of his shirt. He didn't know why he worked so hard on this place. Though he planned to sell the farm soon, he labored as if he planned to stay forever. It just wasn't in him to do anything halfheartedly. But there was nothing for him here now. He wasn't interested in any of the marriageable young women in his *Gmay*. And even if he was, he didn't know how he could open his heart again and let his guard down enough to fall in love with one of them. It hurt too much.

Once he was satisfied the irrigation ditch would run smoothly through the field, he walked to the south pasture. Several fence posts had fallen over, dragging the strands of barbed wire with them. A good farmer always kept his fences mended. Fences helped create good neighbors. But as he dug deeper post holes, he lost his sense of urgency. The *Englisch* farmer bordering his property had no cattle in his field this year and he wondered why. Again, Jonah thought it was such a waste. If he could buy the land, he'd put it to good use. But then he reminded himself he was leaving soon.

He reseated the posts before tamping them firmly into the damp soil. Then he restrung the barbed wire and tacked it into place. Within an hour, his work was finished. He looked up at the sky. The position of the sun and his rumbling stomach told him it was midday. Time to go in for lunch. And then he'd drive Lovina over to get her goats. He didn't mind so much except he never knew what to say to her during the journey.

Packing up his tools, he carried them back to the barn. As he walked, his gaze took in the status of his farm with the critical eye of a meticulous farmer. He scanned the fences for any more breakage. He noticed the outbuildings and his cattle grazing in the east pasture. His milk cows stood in the corral, chewing their cud and swishing their long tails. His two roan draft horses stood grazing beneath the stand of leafless poplar trees near the house. All his livestock appeared strong and healthy. And yet there was much work to do this winter if he was to prepare for spring planting. And since he didn't plan to be here then, he figured he'd do the work for the next farmer who bought this place.

Lovina's goats stayed close to the barn, eating everything in their path. That was good, to a certain extent. They kept the weeds mowed down but sometimes got into other trouble, such as breaking down the fence and wandering up onto the dangerous county road. The chickens pecked around in the yard while the pigs snorted and lounged in the cool dirt of their pen. Everything looked in good order. Though his farm was small, it was tidy and well-kept. The Realtor thought it would sell for a good price.

A flash of lavender caught Jonah's eye and he jerked his head in that direction. Lovina stood in the vegetable garden, her slender back bent as she gathered up tomato gates and stacked them neatly in the gardening shed. She raked compost into the furrows, then stood straight and arched her back before returning to her work. He'd thought about tending to the garden but never needed to do so. Lovina did her chores with an efficiency his farmer's mind could admire. And though he'd tried to grow tomatoes last year, he had to admit no one in the area grew plants as big or as nice as hers. With their cooler, shorter growing season, it was difficult at best. Maybe that was a topic he could address on their trip to buy the new goats. He could ask her to tell him the secret to growing good tomato plants in Colorado.

As he arrived at the barn, he saw Lovina lean her hoe and rake against the back door. She didn't seem to notice him as she went inside. No doubt Autumn was down for her morning nap. Jonah knew Lovina wouldn't leave the baby unattended for long.

Thinking how conscientious Lovina was about her duties, he washed up in the water barrel outside, letting the cold water invigorate him. Then he joined his grandfather in the *dawdi haus* for a lunch of ham sandwiches on store-bought bread. A part of him wished he was eating Lovina's food but it was best to keep his distance right now.

"Did you get the fence repaired?" *Dawdi* asked as he took a bite of his sandwich.

"Ja," Jonah grunted.

"Did you have any trouble?"

"Ne."

And that was the end of their conversation. Men seemed to say what needed to be said while women liked to chatter endlessly about anything and everything. As he washed a bite of bread down with a cool glass of milk, Jonah tried not to smile. Lovina loved to talk as much as any woman but her conversations were usually tied up with the farm and her clients…topics that interested him, too. And for some reason, he kind of liked listening to her talk, though he'd never admit it out loud.

Looking across the tiny table in the *dawdi haus*, he tried to focus on his grandfather.

"Are you feeling better this afternoon?" he asked.

The old man paused and blinked. "Of course. Why?"

"You weren't feeling well this morning.

You said you didn't want to drive over to the Schwartz farm with Lovina and me."

"*Ach*, I'm feeling fine now but I think I need more rest. I'll stay home today," *Dawdi* said.

Jonah shook his head in confusion. And then a thought occurred to him. Was *Dawdi* purposely trying to get him and Lovina alone together? Had the bishop put *Dawdi* up to this? Because if that was the case, it wasn't going to work.

Soon, Jonah returned to the barn to hitch up the horse and buggy. No doubt Lovina would be ready to leave. She was punctual, organizing her day to accommodate her expectant mothers. And though he admired many of her qualities, Jonah dreaded the trip to the Schwartz farm. Because he'd have to spend several hours with Lovina. Alone. But that wasn't the biggest problem. Her lilting laughter sounded so sweet that he wanted to smile and talk with her. But he couldn't allow himself to be taken in by her beguiling ways. The price was too high. He was not interested in her or any woman. No, not ever again.

Chapter Four

By late morning, Lovina was ready to leave. Dressed warmly, she wrapped Autumn in an extra blanket. Because of her profession, Lovina had plenty of diapers and clothes on hand...for a newborn. But the little girl was growing fast and would soon need a larger size.

Carrying the baby against her shoulder, Lovina retrieved her diaper bag and went outside. The day was bright but the north breeze brought a distinct chill to the air. As she crossed the spacious driveway, Lovina shielded the baby's face from the cold wind.

Inside the barn, she found Jonah. He was just finishing up harnessing the horse to the buggy and hadn't noticed Lovina. She watched him work, noticing how his high forehead creased in concentration as he straightened the traces. A spray of dazzling sunlight pierced the shadows of the barn, landing squarely on his broad shoulders and head. She listened as he spoke softly to the horse, telling him what a fine animal he was. That touched her heart like nothing else could. She remembered the bishop saying once that you could tell the caliber of a man by how he treated his animals.

Jonah ran a hand over the horse's neck and shoulder, tugging gently on the collar to ensure it was firmly in position. It was a restful moment and she hated to disturb him. His profile looked lean and firm, his strong, capable hands threading the last leather strap through a buckle. Then he turned and saw her standing in the doorway with the baby. All at once, his expression changed. His lips tilted upward just a bit and she thought he almost smiled. Almost. But then the expression was gone, so fast she thought she must have imagined it.

"*Guder mariye*. Are you ready to go?" he asked, his words low and matter-of-fact.

Gone was the quiet, almost reverent voice he'd used to speak to the horse. Now he sounded a bit gruff and showed not a single hint of enthusiasm for their task ahead.

"I am. But I don't want to put you out. I can go alone. I think Autumn and I will be safe."

She stepped over to the buggy, trying not to show her hurt feelings.

"*Ne*, I will drive you."

It wasn't so much his words but the way he said them. As if it were a command. And that made Lovina bristle. She was an independent woman who worked and paid her own way. She didn't like taking orders from anyone.

As Jonah opened the door, he took the diaper bag from her arm. Using both hands to cradle the baby, she forced herself not to flinch when Jonah clasped her elbow as she climbed inside.

"*Danke.*" She spoke rather coolly, settling into the passenger seat. He handed her the diaper bag and she set it in the middle of the seat. It was a good barrier between them.

As he walked around the buggy and climbed into the driver's seat, she ignored him by fussing with the baby's knit cap. Maybe it had been a bad idea to ask for help on this errand but it would be difficult for her to tend Autumn, drive the buggy and deal with obstinate goats at the same time. And the bishop made it clear he wanted Jonah to accompany her on all her errands. Just now, Autumn was fast asleep and there wasn't much to do. Finally, Lovina sat still as Jonah took the leather leads into his hands, released the brake and urged the horse forward.

Soon they were moving down the dirt road at a fast trot. They didn't speak as they pulled onto the paved county road. The movement of the buggy increased the breeze that whispered past her window and she reached up to ensure it was closed all the way. Fields of drab brown and yellow opened up to Lovina's view, along with black-and-white cows grazing contentedly beside Cherry Creek as it meandered across Jonah's farm. Sedges and sticks of cattail lined the creek. Clusters of trees edged the roadside, their gold, red and brown leaves sparkling against a cerulean sky. It was beautiful here and she wished she could stay in her rented farmhouse forever. But all things came to an end and she knew she would have to leave one day, when Jonah took a wife.

Three miles outside of town, they rounded a bend and Lovina caught sight of a lone Amish woman walking alongside the road. Carrying a wicker basket, she was dressed much like Lovina in a blue skirt, warm winter shawl and starched prayer *kapp*.

"Who is that?" Lovina asked, not recognizing the stranger. She glanced at Jonah and immediately noticed how his shoulders stiffened, his spine rigid and straight.

Lovina looked back at the woman and narrowed her eyes. It couldn't be, could it? Yes, it was!

"It's Fannie." Lovina spoke the obvious.

From the purse of displeasure on Jonah's lips, he'd already recognized his ex-fiancée. It wasn't surprising for the young woman to be here. After all, she lived with her new husband and his parents on their farm no more than a mile down the road.

As they drew closer, Lovina made a pretense of adjusting the baby in her arms. Jonah didn't decrease speed and she wondered if he would just blast right on past. Surely he wouldn't be so rude.

"You should ask if she needs a ride," Lovina said.

Out of her peripheral vision, she thought he rolled his eyes but when she glanced his way, he looked completely neutral. And yet there was a subtle tensing of his hands around the lead lines. It wasn't as if he was irritated but rather uneasy by this chance encounter. Even so, he slowed the horse as Fannie glanced over her shoulder and turned to face them.

Jonah pulled the buggy to a stop along the shoulder of the road.

Shielding the baby from the cool air, Lovina opened her window halfway. *"Hallo!"* she called with a wave.

"Guder mariye!" Fannie returned, her voice vibrating with excitement. Her gaze took them in and, once she recognized Jonah, she showed a nervous smile.

Jonah tugged respectfully on the brim of his hat but didn't look at her nor speak a word. And considering this was the girl who had shattered his heart, Lovina thought he was doing an admirable job of being polite. After all, the tenets of their faith dictated tolerance and love. Even if Fannie had broken off their engagement, the Lord expected Jonah to behave with a forgiving heart and realize that something better awaited him. But from the way he avoided Fannie's eyes, Lovina got the impression his faith wasn't coming easy for him today. And for some odd reason, that caused a surge of compassion to rise in her chest. She felt sorry for him. After all, she knew firsthand what it felt like to suffer a broken heart.

"Can we offer you a ride *heemet*?" Lovina asked the girl.

Fannie's eyes crinkled as she thought this over. Standing rigidly beside the buggy, she shook her head. *"Ne*, I better not. I only have a short way to go. I cut across the field and take a shortcut. It's faster than driving all the way around."

Lovina cringed. "You'll be careful of snakes as you go, won't you?"

Fannie's eyes rounded. "Snakes?"

Lovina shook her head, immediately regretting she'd mentioned it. "Probably not. I'm sure they're hibernating right now."

A strand of brown hair had come undone from Fannie's white prayer *kapp*. She tucked it back in place, looking at the field. "Do you really think so?"

"*Ja*, I'm sure of it. It's too cold for them now," Lovina said.

Fannie hesitated, as if she might change her mind and ask for a ride anyway. But one glance at Jonah and his stony profile nixed that. He didn't say a word as he stared straight ahead. He seemed so tense. Lovina wondered if he'd forgiven Fannie for ending their engagement. The thought that he might be harboring resentment toward the girl made Lovina sad. No doubt it had been difficult for him to attend Fannie's marriage to Alvin Fisher five months earlier. To top it off, Jonah now had to endure seeing the couple together at their church and social gatherings, gushing over each other as newlyweds were prone to do. If that were the case, Jonah must still love the girl, a thought that bothered Lovina even more, though she couldn't say why.

Fannie's gaze swept over the sleeping baby. "*Ach*, what a sweet little cutie-pie. Whose *boppli* do you have there?"

Autumn's small face was turned slightly toward Jonah as she breathed between parted rosebud lips. Lovina explained what she'd carefully rehearsed about the baby, then endured several minutes of endearments as Fannie admired the tiny girl.

"*Ach*, she's so precious. I hope her *mudder* feels better soon," Fannie said.

"*Ja*, I hope so, too," Lovina agreed.

There was a long pause after Lovina asked about Fannie's *familye*. Jonah continued to sit in silence.

"Everyone is *gut* at home, except Alvin has a terrible head cold," Fannie said.

"*Ach*, are you sure it's a cold? It might be allergies. Ragweed and sage are bad this time of year," Lovina said.

Fannie shrugged, looking a bit helpless. "I have no idea. I don't know what to do for him. He's so miserable. His throat is sore and his nose runs all the time."

Lovina reached out and placed a comforting hand on Fannie's arm, trying to offer reassurance. Everyone in their *Gmay* knew Fannie was normally a bit nervous. Some people were naturally higher-strung than others. But she also was one of the first to volunteer to help when the need arose.

"Give him lots of liquids and have him gargle with salt water. That might help. I hope he's feeling better soon," Lovina said.

Fannie's eyes widened. "Do you think so? *Ja*, I'll try that. *Danke*!"

"We'd best be moving on now." Jonah spoke low and started the buggy moving while Fannie still leaned against the side.

Taking the hint, she stepped back. "*Ach*, of course. See you at church then."

With a curt nod, Jonah slapped the lines against the horse's back and the animal moved off at a quick trot. As she closed the window, Lovina watched Fannie in the rear-view mirror. The young woman turned toward the open field bordering her husband's property and finally disappeared from view. Lovina frowned. She noticed a dark scowl tugged at Jonah's forehead as he took the turn leading to the Schwartzes' farm where they would buy the goats.

After a moment, Lovina spoke. "That was rude and unkind."

Jonah just grunted, knowing full well what

she was talking about. "I thought we should get on with our day."

"It never would have worked out," she said.

"What?"

"Marrying Fannie. She was never the right girl for you," she said.

He glanced her way, his eyes flashing with annoyance. "Why not?"

Lovina waved one hand in the air. "The two of you aren't compatible. You have completely different personalities."

"What do you mean?" he asked.

Oh, dear. He sounded peeved and Lovina wondered if she should end this conversation right now. And yet something spurred her onward. As if her own future happiness relied upon what she was about to say.

"You obviously still harbor harsh feelings toward Fannie," she pointed out.

He didn't respond, just glowered at the road.

"The Lord wants us all to have a forgiving heart. It brings us lasting peace," she continued.

She wasn't sure but thought she heard him release a low growl. And rather than frighten her, she almost laughed out loud.

"Fannie is pretty and sweet but remember how she fell to pieces at the fall social when she saw a spider?" Lovina couldn't forget the girl's high-pitched screams. They still rang in her ears. "On the other hand, you're quiet and solemn all the time. The two of you are completely wrong for each other. You're not compatible."

He shrugged one powerful shoulder. "I don't know. I've heard that opposites attract. Maybe that's why we became a couple in the first place."

Lovina had her doubts but didn't voice them.

"And anyway, what makes you such an expert on the topic of matchmaking?" he asked.

She'd touched a raw nerve. The last thing she wanted was to hurt his feelings.

"You're right. I'm no expert. Please forgive me and forget I ever mentioned it," she said.

He pursed his lips and tossed her a frown that could have shriveled onions. They rode in silence for several long minutes. Then…

"You really think I'm solemn?" Jonah asked.

Lovina nodded. "*Ja*, I do. You rarely smile and sometimes your expression looks hard as a block of stone. It wouldn't hurt you to laugh once in a while, you know?"

Her comments won her an even stonier expression.

"I'm a grown man, not a child to run around laughing all the time. I've got heavy responsibilities," he said.

"True, but you should still smile now and then," she said.

Yes, he was definitely a grown man. And the meticulous way he took care of his farm told her that Fannie's penchant for constant reassurance would have grated on his nerves before too long. And though Lovina didn't say that, she sensed he knew it already. She hesitated, her brain churning for something positive to say.

"The Lord wants us to have joy, but being sober isn't all bad either," she said. "You strike me as a serious man who is calm and self-assured. You know who you are and what you want, and you work hard to get it. Your farm is a prime example of that. But Fannie is rather, um…"

He dipped his head in acceptance. "*Ja*, she can be a little bit…" He hesitated, as if searching for the right word.

"Fussy? Fearful?" Lovina offered.

He snorted. "I was going to say anxious. But she's rather fastidious, too. Her *heemet* is quite tidy. I like that."

Yes, he would. But Fannie was also high maintenance. She seemed to need a lot of reassurance. Some people were inherently like that. But Lovina didn't say anything else. It wouldn't be kind, especially since Lovina had so many faults of her own. It was enough that Jonah recognized these things. And if he couldn't see that Fannie was completely wrong for him and would have made him unhappy, it wasn't Lovina's place to point it out to him. Especially since the girl was now married to someone else. But maybe this conversation would help Jonah feel better about the breakup. Or maybe it would make him feel worse. Lovina wasn't sure. And as they drove into the narrow yard at the Schwartzes' farm, she wondered why she even cared.

Jonah pulled the horse and buggy to a halt just in front of Mervin Schwartz's big gray pole barn. The man stood in the middle of the driveway with his wife, Hannah, and one of their teenage daughters. Good! Mervin was at home. Jonah had feared the farmer might be out working in his fields.

Mervin waved and walked toward them. Jonah climbed out of the buggy and hurried around to assist Lovina and the baby. As he helped them down, he thought about what Lovina said about Fannie. He didn't agree with her assessment of his ex-fiancée at all.

Yes, Fannie could be overly sensitive and excitable at times but she was also sweet, kind and considerate of others' needs. And she made the best schnitz apple pie he'd ever tasted. No one was perfect all the time, including him. But as he walked with Lovina to meet Mervin and Hannah Schwartz, Jonah couldn't help wondering if maybe his love for Fannie had caused him to overlook a few of her flaws that might have irked him over time. But wasn't that what love was supposed to do? Jesus Christ's entire mission was to forgive all failings, if only we would repent of our sins. And yet Jonah couldn't help wondering about Lovina's assessment.

You're not compatible.

Jonah had never heard anything so outrageous. He'd grown up believing love could conquer all. What did it have to do with being compatible? If they both loved and served the Lord and loved each other, that was enough. Wasn't it?

"*Hallo!* What brings you out to our place this fine day?" Mervin boomed in his energetic bass voice.

Jonah inwardly smiled. He'd always liked this gregarious man. Mervin was just as loud and boisterous as his wife was quiet and meek. And Jonah longed to point out to

Lovina that the Schwartzes were complete opposites, too, yet they'd made a fine marriage with lots of active children.

"Guder nummidaag." Lovina wished them a good afternoon, her voice filled with eager anticipation. "I'm hoping you might have some goats you can sell me."

Mervin jerked a thumb toward his wife. *"Ach,* that's Hannah's area. She takes care of the goats on our place. I just keep them fed."

Hannah stepped forward, gravitating toward Autumn. *"Ja,* I've got goats you can buy. But first, who is this little one you're holding?"

Lovina quickly explained and soon handed the baby over to Hannah for her to hold.

"Komm and I'll show you the goats I have to sell." Carrying Autumn securely in her arms, Hannah headed over to the expansive pen where the active animals were kept.

Jonah and Mervin followed as Lovina studied the herd milling around the feeding troughs. From past experience, he knew the goats were pint-sized dynamos that stood no more than twenty-five inches tall and came in an assortment of gold, chocolate, black and multicolor. They bleated and hopped around the yard, their ears long, their short tails held high like mini flags. Though Jonah liked sheep and lambies, he loved goats and their happy zest for life. And a part of him was glad Lovina liked goats, too.

"My goats are great workhorses," Hannah said. "They give lots of milk, make lots of compost for your garden, and they're friendly to *kinder*, too. How many do you need?"

"Could I buy two?" Lovina asked.

Hannah nodded and waved a hand at the herd. "Certainly! Take your pick."

The woman opened the gate and let Lovina step inside the pasture. Jonah and Mervin followed but Hannah stayed back and closed the gate since she was still holding Autumn.

Jonah waited as Lovina studied the goats. He wanted to see which ones she chose. He would soon know if she had a good eye for healthy animals or not, which was important to a farmer like him.

He watched as her gaze scoured the herd. There were several young animals with soft coats, bright, inquisitive eyes, trimmed hooves, slim and friendly. Lovina seemed to be focused on a black-and-white female and a golden one, which impressed Jonah. They were the exact two goats he would have picked.

Lovina pointed. "How about those two? Whoa!"

Before he could react, Lovina was thrown fully against Jonah's chest. In an automatic response, he reached out to steady her. An older, obstinate goat had butted her from behind and knocked her forward.

"Oof!" he grunted, his arms wrapped around her so she didn't fall.

"Oh!" she cried.

She slumped against him, trying to regain her footing. And when she did, he found himself staring down into her brilliant blue eyes. She stood there for several pounding seconds, locked in his embrace. For what seemed an eternity, he felt transfixed by time. He couldn't move. Couldn't breathe. Finally, he forced himself to inhale, desperate to regain his composure. And in those scant moments, he was conscious that she smelled of lemon soap and fresh-baked bread, a combination he found strangely attractive and exhilarating.

"I... I'm sorry!" she exclaimed, taking a step back.

He let her go, his face hot. Out of the corner of his eye, he saw Mervin and Hannah watching them and smiling.

"*Ach*, are you *allrecht*?" Mervin asked Lovina.

"*Ja*, I'm fine. I guess the goats got the better of me," Lovina responded with a laugh, her voice sounding abnormally shaky as she rubbed her posterior where the goat had struck her.

"They'll do that when you least expect it," Hannah said, still wearing a cheery smile. "You know, I just have to say that you two make such a darling couple. Dare I hope for another wedding soon?"

Lovina's mouth dropped open in shock. Her face mirrored what Jonah felt. After informing him that he and Fannie were completely ill-suited, he wasn't in the mood to hear such a thing. Not when he considered Lovina to be the most incompatible woman in their *Gmay* because of her past.

"Oh, we aren't… I mean…we're not…" Lovina stammered, as if she were unable to complete a coherent thought.

Hannah shared a knowing look with her husband, then nodded her head. "Maybe not now, but you two sure are cute together."

Cute! Jonah took a sharp inhale.

Mervin glanced at him. "*Ja*, you should ask her out sometime. You don't want her to get away."

Jonah coughed. He'd never heard such an absurd idea in all his life. Lovina was the last woman he wanted to date. But he wasn't about to let this topic continue. Turning toward Lovina, he pointed at the two goats he thought she wanted to buy.

"Are those the ones you like?" he growled, irritated beyond words.

"*Ja*, I... I'll take them," she stammered, looking as dismayed as he felt.

Walking to the gate, she let herself out of the pasture and reached to take Autumn from Hannah's arms. Jonah forced himself to act pleasant as Mervin helped him catch the two goats. With a rope tied around their necks, Jonah stoically led them out of the pen and tied them behind the buggy. With the patience of Job, he waited for Lovina to pay Hannah the required fee. The two women laughed and chatted for several minutes. A part of him admitted it wasn't Mervin and Hannah's fault he was annoyed and bewildered right now. But inside, he was screaming. There wasn't one single woman in this *Gmay* that he would consider marrying. And he didn't have to look twice at Lovina's expression to know she felt the same about him. Which suited him just fine. Because he was leaving this place as soon as he could sell his farm and was never coming back.

Chapter Five

Three days later, Lovina pushed open the screen door and stepped out onto Abby Fisher's front porch. Birds twittered in the tall poplars lining the front yard. The tree limbs had dropped their leaves. Jakob, Abby's husband, had raked two hours earlier and the air smelled of damp, loamy soil. This was Lovina's second and last prenatal visit of the day, and she was eager to get home to the chores waiting for her there. Holding her medical bag, she shielded her eyes from the late-morning sun.

"*Danke* for coming to see me today." Abby, one of Lovina's expectant mothers, followed her outside.

"You're *willkomm*," Lovina said.

She paused as Abby let the screen door clap closed behind them. Lovina had arrived at the farmhouse forty minutes earlier for a prenatal visit for a new pregnancy. As usual, Jonah had driven her here. She'd visited Norma Albrecht earlier. Now that the new mother was out of the hospital, it was time for her postnatal follow-ups. Soon, Lovina would be finished with her rounds and could take Autumn home.

"And you take these little clothes. They no longer fit my Christine. Maybe you can use them for Autumn."

Abby handed Lovina two bags of baby clothes. Though they were used, they were almost like new and Lovina was more than grateful.

"*Ach*, that's so kind of you. I'll return them as soon as she doesn't need them anymore," Lovina promised.

A spear of delight pierced her chest. She'd been planning to make more clothes for Autumn and wondered when she'd find the time. Then she thought she might need to ask Jonah to drive her into town to shop for some little garments. No doubt he would just loooove making another trip with her. That thought brought a smile to her lips. He always obliged her even though he didn't seem to like it. Thankfully, Abby's generosity saved him the trouble.

"I heard Norma Albrecht is out of the hospital. But I guess you already know that," Abby said.

"*Ja*, I saw her this morning, right before I came over here. Her baby boy is awfully sweet and so alert," Lovina said.

"Have they decided on a name for him, yet?"

Lovina nodded. "Ephraim."

"*Ach*, that's a fine name." Abby smiled, then glanced up. "I wonder where our men have gone off to."

Our men! A flush of heat suffused Lovina's face. Jonah wasn't her man. But pointing that out to Abby would only make the moment more uncomfortable.

Lovina scanned the yard, searching for some sight of Jonah and Abby's husband. While Lovina had given Abby a prenatal exam and drawn some blood for lab work, Jonah had remained outside with Autumn. It was warm enough that she didn't need her coat but Lovina knew that wouldn't last. Any day now, they could get their first snowstorm of the season. The fact that Jonah had offered to tend to the child while Lovina was occupied had impressed her. But now she felt a bit anxious, knowing Autumn would need a bottle soon.

Stepping off the porch, Lovina walked toward the graveled driveway where Jonah's horse and buggy stood waiting beneath the expanse of several willow trees. Abby accompanied her, the ribbons to her white prayer *kapp* fluttering in the light breeze.

"There they are!" Abby pointed toward the trees.

The two men stood on the far side of the buggy. Jakob was holding Christine, his two-and-a-half-year-old daughter. The child was dressed identical to her mother, her tiny white prayer *kapp* indicating she was a girl.

Jonah had his back turned toward the women. As usual, he swayed gently back and forth as he cradled Autumn in the crook of his arm. His head was tilted slightly as he listened intently to what Jakob was saying. From that gesture alone, Lovina could tell he was actively involved in the conversation. If he held his head aloft and looked away, she knew he was distracted and wanted to be somewhere else. And she couldn't help wondering how she'd learned that about this man.

Seeing the two women, Jakob smiled wide. "*Hallo*! Is all well?"

Abby went to stand beside her husband. He gazed down at her, a look of concern and adoration in his eyes that spoke volumes. It was clear this man dearly loved his wife.

"*Ja*, all is well," Abby spoke in a shy whisper and nodded. Christine reached for her mommy, and Abby took her into her arms before kissing the girl's forehead.

Fearing the bit of breeze was too much for Autumn, Lovina tugged a corner of the blanket up to protect the baby's face. Then she reached into the buggy and took out a small brown paper sack, which she handed to Abby.

"These are the red raspberry leaves I told you about," she said. "I dry them myself every year. Just put a tablespoon or so in your herbal tea to steep and then drink it all down. I think it should help ease your morning sickness."

Abby took the bag and rested one hand briefly over her flat stomach. She was barely two months along. "*Danke*, I appreciate it. I didn't have a bit of sickness with Christine. Jakob's *mudder* thinks this new *boppli* must be a boy to make me feel so unwell all the time."

"Boys will do that," Lovina quipped.

Abby gave a nervous laugh, but Lovina saw a flicker of doubt in the woman's eyes. While the young mother had an active toddler at home, she had suffered a miscarriage last spring and was eager to carry this new child to term.

Jakob smiled at Lovina, his expression one of gratitude. "If not for your help, I don't know what we would have done. You've been there with us through it all."

His words touched Lovina's heart. Coming from a father, the compliment was extra special. Lovina didn't speak but merely slanted her head, forcing herself not to feel pride. As Abby's midwife, it was Lovina's job to look after her, including her emotional and psychological needs. But perhaps because she had lost a child of her own, Lovina had taken Abby's miscarriage quite personally, and she desperately wanted this new pregnancy to be a success.

Jakob put a protective arm around his wife's shoulders and leaned closer to her. Without a word, he conveyed his sympathy and loving support. Lovina watched the caring gesture with eagle eyes. And though it was against her faith to feel envy, Lovina couldn't help being a little jealous of the couple's caring relationship. How she wished there was one man somewhere in the world who loved her the way Jakob loved Abby.

Reaching out, Lovina squeezed Abby's hand with warm affection. "*Ach*, your morning sickness should pass within a few weeks. And while I know it makes you feel awful, the nausea is a symptom of a healthy, viable pregnancy. So as long as you're able to keep enough food down and retain your strength, I take this as a *gut* sign."

"Do you really think so?" Abby asked, her eyes filled with uncertainty.

Lovina thought about the medical studies she'd read recently on the topic but she didn't mention them to Abby. The Amish didn't teach science in their parochial schools or put much store in the subject. Rather, they put their faith in *Gott*.

"I know so," she said. "There is definitely a lower rate of miscarriage with women who suffer from nausea in their early months. I have every reason to believe you'll carry this *boppli* to term."

Abby breathed a little sigh and showed a smile of relief. "Oh, *danke*, Lovina! That's the best news I've heard all week." She tilted her face toward her husband. "Isn't that *wundervoll*, Jakob?"

"*Ja*, it's tremendous news," he said, returning her smile.

Lovina felt the love between them. There was such adulation in their gazes that Lovina's chest tightened. Again, she longed to experience such a caring relationship. A husband and *familye* of her own was all she'd ever wanted. But after what she'd done, she doubted any man could forgive her actions. So, hoping for something that could never be was torturous to her heart and she pushed it aside.

"And if you run out of raspberry leaves, just let me know. I've got plenty more," she said.

Abby nodded and their conversation lagged. Jonah shifted his weight, a movement that told Lovina he felt a bit uncomfortable with this intimate conversation. The married couple didn't seem to notice Jonah's unease but Lovina did. She was getting to know him quite well and was highly aware of his moods. He stepped back and shaded his eyes as he peered up at the gathering clouds.

"*Ach*, we may awaken to snow in the morning," he said.

The change of topic was obvious to Lovina. She knew both men must feel a tad uncomfortable to be talking about Abby's condition. Normally, the Amish didn't verbally acknowledge pregnancy until the baby was born. But Jonah was an EMT and Lovina was Abby's midwife, so it was her job to discuss such personal matters with this married couple. The loss of their last child had been a difficult blow for Abby to bear, and Lovina knew the couple was inordinately pleased by today's good news.

So was Lovina.

"*Ja*, we'd best get going and let you move on with your day," Lovina said.

Abby reached up and gently patted Autumn's small back. "I know you'll take *gut* care of this little one until her *mamm* is feeling well enough to be back with her soon."

A part of Lovina hoped so but another part prayed the missing mother was never found. She just nodded as Jonah opened the buggy door and she climbed inside. He handed Autumn up to her, then walked around to the driver's seat. With a wave of his hand, Jonah urged the horse into a trot down the lane. Abby and Jakob stood there watching them go, their arms twined behind each other's backs with little Christine cuddled between them.

Jonah had turned onto the county road leading home before either of them spoke.

"Did Abby ask you any questions about where Autumn came from?" Jonah asked.

"*Ja*, she wanted to know who the baby belonged to," Lovina said.

"And?"

Lovina shrugged. "And I told her what we'd agreed to say. That Autumn's *mudder* isn't feeling well and I'm looking after the *boppli* for the time being."

He nodded his approval and, though Lovina knew he was just looking after Autumn's best interests, his questions irritated her. It was as if he didn't trust her judgment. After all, she was a strong, independent woman and didn't need Jonah's approval for anything. She could handle this situation on her own. But she realized needing someone had nothing to do with the deep desires of her heart.

"Did Abby want to know anything else about Autumn?" Jonah asked.

"Ne," she snapped a bit too harshly, and quickly softened her tone. After all, it wasn't Jonah's fault people were curious about the baby. "Abby accepted my explanation without objection or any overt curiosity. In fact, you're asking me more questions than she did."

That won a quick look from Jonah. He blinked, as if surprised by her waspish tongue.

"I know you're a highly capable midwife," he conceded, his voice conciliatory. "I didn't mean offense. I'm just trying to protect you and the *boppli*, as the bishop asked me to."

Great! Now Lovina felt rotten for letting her temper get the better of her. She told herself she was being overly sensitive, and yet this man made her feel like she needed to defend herself all the time. He made her feel… angry and resentful. And that was contrary to what *Gott* wanted from her. She must be more patient, long-suffering and slow to take offense. There was absolutely no reason for her to be defensive every time she was around Jonah. None at all.

"I'm sorry. I didn't mean to bite at you like that," she said.

He ducked his head and stared forward, navigating the road as he drove them home. They rode in heavy silence for several minutes, and Lovina felt at a loss for words. She longed to tell Jonah how bad she felt that they weren't better friends. There was so much she wanted to say to him. Things she wished she could confide. If only she knew what to say to help them get past the invisible brick wall standing between them. But what good would that do? Jonah must accept her for who she was. Because she couldn't change her past and there was nothing she could say to alter his opinion of her. And that was that.

"I didn't mean to upset you," Jonah spoke several minutes later.

He didn't look at Lovina but kept his gaze

on the road. He sensed his questions made her angry, though that had never been his intent. Only her tart response gave him any clue as to what she was thinking.

"Forget it," she said, her small jaw locked in a stubborn scowl.

Hmm. If only he could forget. It certainly wasn't Lovina's fault his mother and Fannie had left him. Lovina's past wasn't his business, either. It was between her and the Lord. And yet he found himself wishing he could trust her. Wishing things could be different between them. But that didn't diminish his resolve to sell his farm and move back east.

"*Ach*, look!" Lovina pointed at the side of the road.

Jonah jerked his head in that direction, expecting to see some amazing sight. But he saw nothing more than a thatch of burdock plants lining the fence. Their bright pink flowers and prickly heads waved in the morning breeze.

"*Schtopp*, please," she cried.

He did so, thinking he must not see what she found so interesting. What on earth did she want with common burdock plants?

When he put on the brake, she handed him the baby.

"I'll be right back," she said.

Pulling a paper sack out of the large bag she'd stowed on the back seat, she got out of the buggy with quick agility. As she neared the field, she hopped over a trickling stream of water and daintily picked her way over to the barbed wire fence. Cradling the baby in his arms, Jonah watched Lovina's every move, just in case she needed help. But if anything, he'd learned this woman was quite self-sufficient and dynamic. The complete opposite of Fannie. And though he didn't expect to feel this way, Jonah kind of liked that about Lovina.

She approached the patch of burdock. The plants were over four feet tall and had large, heart-shaped leaves the size of his outstretched hand. The pink flowers and cockleburs were in full bloom. Though they could appear quite pretty, he hated the obnoxious plants and watched in horror as she began to pluck the leaves and carefully stow them inside her sack.

"Leave them! What on earth do you want those for?" he called through the open window, thinking she'd lost her mind.

As a farmer, he had no use for the nasty weeds and was grateful he had none to contaminate his farm. Over the years, he'd spent hours pulling the irritating cockleburs off the eyelashes, tails and hides of his livestock after they'd gotten into the irksome plants. He could say nothing good about them. Why Lovina wanted the deep green leaves, he had no idea.

Having quickly filled her bag, she headed back toward him, lifting her long skirts out of the way as she again jumped the stream. As she ran toward the buggy, he couldn't help thinking she was a spunky little thing. So determined and full of life.

She fell! She disappeared completely from sight.

Jonah gasped and sat up straighter, holding the baby a bit tighter. He waited for Lovina to stand but she simply sat up. Through the thick weeds and brush covering the side of the road, he could see no more than her head and shoulders.

She turned toward him, a grimace of pain covering her pretty face. And Jonah waited no longer.

Bundling the baby up, he flipped an edge of the blanket over her head to protect her face from the chilly air and climbed out of the buggy. With long strides, he reached Lovina's side.

"Are you *allrecht*?" he asked.

She sat in the middle of the sedge grass,

rubbing her ankle with both hands. Her sack of burdock leaves lay forgotten at her side.

"I… I think so. I twisted my ankle." Her voice trembled and he knew she was in pain.

Kneeling down, he handed Autumn to her. "Here! Hold the *boppli*."

He didn't wait to explain as she took the child into her arms and buried her face in the warmth of the blanket. Jonah hoped she wasn't crying. More than anything, he hated to see a woman cry.

With both hands, he gently inspected Lovina's ankle. He squeezed and checked the soundness of the bone. Through her black stockings, her skin felt warm against his palms.

"I don't believe it's broken. Do you think you can stand?" he asked.

She lifted her head and nodded readily. As he helped her up, he noticed her eyes were red and she bit her bottom lip, as if refusing to cry. She was a gutsy gal, he'd give her that.

"Oh!" she cried out when she tried to put weight on her foot. She winced and stumbled. He shot out his arms to steady her, making a snap judgment right then and there.

"Hold tight to the *boppli*," he said before reaching toward her.

"*Ach*, please don't forget my sack of leaves!"

she cried, and pointed to where it lay upon the ground.

Shaking his head in annoyance, he quickly snatched up the bag and handed it to her, then he picked her up. She inhaled a sudden breath, but he ignored her look of surprise and carried her toward the buggy. With the baby in her arms, she couldn't very well refuse him. She felt light and warm in his arms, and he caught her fragrance of fresh baked bread and baby lotion. As long as he lived, he would associate those two aromas with Lovina. And for some reason, that made him feel bright and happy inside.

"I… I can walk on my own two feet." She spoke with outraged indignation.

"*Ne*, you can't. You've injured your ankle, and I can't leave you sitting out here all day long. It's getting colder, and I need to get you and the *boppli heemet*," he insisted. He refused to meet her gaze, but out of his peripheral vision, he caught her exasperated expression.

As he carried the two of them, he felt Lovina's breath against his cheek. Holding her this close made him feel a sense of purpose he didn't understand or even want to contemplate. Never had he felt so strong and invincible. Like he could do anything. A surge of protective strength rose up within him, and he thought there was almost nothing he wouldn't do to keep this woman and baby safe from harm.

Thankfully, Lovina stopped fighting him. It didn't take long until he had both her and the baby safely inside the buggy. Jonah could just imagine what the bishop would say if he heard that he'd had to bring Lovina and Autumn up the embankment. But Jonah figured that was better than making Lovina walk and possibly injure her ankle more. Since Bishop Yoder had assigned him to protect Lovina and Autumn, he was determined to use his best judgment and do just that. And right now, that meant he had to carry Lovina when she couldn't walk on her own.

Reaching to the back seat, Jonah retrieved a heavy quilt he kept there for emergencies.

"Wrap this around yourself and the *boppli*. I don't want either of you to get cold," he said.

Lovina didn't argue as she did just that. Though the baby seemed fine, Lovina was shivering. Her cheeks and nose were red and her teeth clacked together. The baby began to fuss and Lovina offered her a bottle as Jonah slapped the lead lines against the horse's rump and they continued on their way home.

"*Ach*, thanks for rescuing me," Lovina said after a few minutes of silence.

"You're *willkomm*. But what was so important about burdock leaves that you had to put yourself through that?" Jonah asked.

Lovina shrugged, her voice vibrating from the cold and excitement. "I dry the leaves, then store them for a later time when they can be useful."

He snorted. "Useful for what? Burdock isn't *gut* for anything, except snagging onto the hides of my cattle and horses."

She laughed, the sound high and sweet. "*Ja*, the cockleburs do stick to everything."

As a case in point, she plucked several of the burs from her long skirt and rolled the window down a teensy bit so she could toss them out.

"Some people use the roots to make an herbal tea," she continued. "I use the leaves to ease the pain of burns and help wounds heal faster."

He stared in awe as she stashed the bag of burdock leaves in the back, then tucked a burp rag beneath the baby's chin to catch the milky drool. Lovina hummed a wordless tune as she rocked the little girl. Autumn gazed up at her, sucking fiercely on the bottle.

Jonah felt a bit foolish. He was an EMT,

after all. He knew quite a bit about the natural remedies his Amish people used on a daily basis for simple aches, pains and bruises. But he'd never heard of using burdock leaves for burns. Lovina had taught him something new today. Not surprising, since he was quickly learning this woman had a vast knowledge of many things. She had an uncanny way of caring about other people. And he realized he liked that about her.

"Is there anything you don't know?" he asked before he thought to stop himself.

She snapped her head up and stared at him with shock. "Of course. I would never presume to know everything. Not at all. Only *Gott* knows all things. I learn something new every day."

So did he, but he wasn't going to admit she'd become one of his greatest teachers. Instead, he merely nodded, impressed by her skills and abilities in spite of his preconceived biases. But that didn't mean they could be any more than friends.

Chapter Six

A light dusting of snow blanketed the ground the following morning. Frost glimmered around the windowpane over the kitchen sink. It was Church Sunday and Lovina was up early, hobbling around the room to feed Autumn and get ready for the long drive out to the Burkholder farm for services. After her accident yesterday, she was moving rather slow.

Thinking about the tumble she'd taken caused her face to flush. When Jonah had carried her and Autumn to the buggy, she'd felt odd and trembly inside—feelings she'd never experienced before. Not a scary thing but rather the opposite. Like everything would be all right, because Jonah was there looking out for her. And now as she contemplated it, she realized she'd felt strangely…

Safe.

Which was something she hadn't felt in years. Especially with a man. And that didn't make sense. Jonah didn't like her. Not really. She sensed it every time he was around. Yet he always made her feel secure, a thought that made her wonder if she was seriously losing her mind.

Reaching inside the fridge for a bottle of goat's milk, she stashed it and several sterilized baby bottles in the diaper bag and turned.

"Oww!" she cried softly as she put too much weight on her injury.

She sank into a chair. Last night, she thought she was fine after placing ice-cold rags against the area, but her ankle had swelled in the night. Though it wasn't broken, it was quite painful. She'd probably torn the tendons and ligaments. How would she get through this day with a baby?

Autumn lay wide-awake in her portable seat on the table. She waved her little arms and made endearing cooing sounds, growing more alert every day. Her pain forgotten, Lovina reached out and rested her hand against the girl's chest. The baby gazed at her with complete trust. So sweet. So innocent and precious. Once Bishop Yoder found her mother, Lovina wondered how she was ever going to give this baby up.

She heaved a weary sigh. So much for making it to church on time. She could barely walk today. And sitting here dawdling didn't help. If that wasn't bad enough, a knock sounded on the back door. The tall shadow through the glass pane told her it was Jonah. Rather than getting up, she called to him.

"Komm in!"

He did so, stepping onto the rag rug just inside as he wiped his feet and closed the door to cut off the chilly draft. In a sweeping gaze, she noticed he wore his best pair of black broadfall pants and Sunday church coat. His hair was damp and carefully combed and his face clean-shaven. She could tell he'd even dusted his black felt hat and shined his boots. And though he worked hard, she liked that he knew how to tidy up when the occasion warranted it.

In a glance, he took in the entire room. Lovina felt uncomfortable beneath his astute gaze as he took in the disorder. She was normally tidy, but not today. A fluffy towel from the baby's bath lay piled in a heap on the table, and Lovina hadn't yet put away the lotion bottle and tiny brush she used to comb Autumn's fine hair. Pans and dishes from processing the morning milk were still stacked in the sink, waiting to be washed. Sterilized bottles and nipples lay air-drying on a rack. At least Lovina was dressed and her hair brushed and pinned beneath her prayer *kapp*, though she doubted she looked very nice since she hadn't slept well.

"*Ach*, are you *allrecht*?" Jonah asked, taking a step forward.

A frown crinkled his brow and she hated for him to see her like this. He already thought the worst of her.

"Of course. I'm fine." She looked away, bracing her hands against the tabletop to help her stand. In doing so, she couldn't contain a slight wince.

"*Ne*, you're not. Your ankle is still sore."

It wasn't a question. As he took her arm and gently pushed her back down into the chair, she wondered why he always seemed so in tune with her feelings.

"Sit. The best thing for you is rest," he said.

"I'm not missing church today. If I don't show up, everyone will talk. You know how they are. They'll all start showing up on my doorstep and then ask even more questions about Autumn," she spoke fast, wishing he'd just ignore her for once.

"Would that be so bad? It seems to me you

need help today. You're injured, so why not take it easy?"

"I don't have time for that right now."

"I can help." He stood towering over her, his hands on his lean hips as he looked down at her with an expression that told her he could be stubborn, too.

Lovina frowned. It wasn't within her to show weakness like this. She hated relying on him, or anyone, for help. Life had taught her to keep to herself. To never trust anyone. Right now, she wished he'd just go away and leave her alone.

"I'm going to church and that's that," she insisted.

His lips twitched and, once again, she thought he might smile. But he didn't.

"*Allrecht*, what needs to be done so we aren't late?" He removed his coat and draped it over the back of a chair. Rolling up the long sleeves of his blue chambray shirt, he stepped over to the sink.

Oh, no! He wasn't going to wash her dishes, was he?

"I can do that later," she said.

Too late! He flipped on the water faucet with a twist of his wrist. Then he reached for the shavings of dish soap she kept in a jar beside the window ledge. Within moments, he'd scattered some into the hot water and whipped them around with a brisk movement of his hand. Sudsy bubbles formed on top.

"I'll get this done for you now. We'll be eating at church, so you won't have to cook today. Then when we come *heemet* this evening, you won't have it waiting for you. Has Autumn eaten yet?" He didn't look at her as he spoke but reached for a pile of plates and pans and submerged them in the soapy water.

"*Ja*, I saw to her needs first." Lovina watched as he washed her dishes with proficient swipes of the dishcloth.

When he was done, he rinsed and stacked them neatly in the drain where they would air-dry. Then he turned, drying off his hands on a dish towel as he scanned the kitchen. "I've already fed your goats and *Dawdi* is gathering the eggs now. What else must be done?"

"Really, you don't need to do any more," she said.

"Of course I do. The bishop asked me to."

The bishop!

A feeling of disappointment rose in her chest. Jonah was simply fulfilling an assignment from the bishop, nothing more. A part of her wished he was helping her because he wanted to and for no other reason.

Lovina licked her lips, her mouth feeling suddenly dry. Of all the men in her *Gmay*, she didn't want to be beholden to this one, mainly because he didn't appear to like her much. But it couldn't be helped now.

"That's it. There's nothing else. *Danke*. You've taken care of everything, it seems." As she reached for the baby's bath towel and draped it over another chair so it would dry, she couldn't help feeling grateful. Fifteen minutes earlier, she'd felt overwhelmed. Now a modicum of order had been restored to her home. But what must he think of her?

"*Gut*! We can go now. You rest here while I get the buggy," he said.

"You're not carrying me again," she said.

He blinked at her. "I don't think that will be necessary."

Rolling the sleeves to his shirt down his long forearms, he shrugged into his coat, then headed out the door, leaving behind a brief blast of chilled air.

Lovina groaned and buried her face in her hands. Of all the stupid things to say. But sitting here feeling sorry for herself wouldn't help. While he was gone, she stood and hopped on one foot as she crossed the room and retrieved her heavy winter shawl. True to his word, Jonah returned moments later with a narrow wooden cane and *Dawdi* Noah. The elderly man was carrying a basket of eggs.

"Jonah told me your predicament. You poor girl. Twisted your ankle, did you?" *Dawdi* glanced at her feet, which were encased in warm black stockings and practical shoes.

Right now, Lovina wished she dared wear her soft slippers instead but figured that would only raise eyebrows at church.

"*Ja*, but I'm sure it's nothing to worry about. I'll be fine tomorrow," Lovina said.

Shaking his head, *Dawdi* simply made a *tsk*ing sound as he opened the fridge door and slid the eggs inside. Lovina made a mental note to clean them later that evening when she got home.

"This is a spare cane *Dawdi* uses sometimes. I think you might need it today." Jonah handed her the sturdy piece of hickory. Without waiting for permission, he reached for the baby.

Heaving a sigh of resignation, Lovina gripped the smooth hilt of the cane as she gingerly put slight weight on her sore ankle. Though it wasn't perfect, the cane did help diminish the pain and she was able to hobble to the door.

"I think this will help me a great deal. *Danke*!" She showed a slight smile and took a quick inhale. Because, wonder of wonders, Jonah smiled back. And the expression lit up his face like nothing else could. For a fraction of a moment, she thought him the most handsome man she'd ever seen. Then his smile dropped away and he turned toward the door.

"*Gut*! Now we can get on with our day. What should I put on the *boppli* to keep her warm?" he asked.

"Her bundling is right there." Lovina pointed to where the fleece bunting with a warm hood was draped over the diaper bag.

Laying the baby gently on a blanket, Jonah leaned over her and slid her down into the bundling bag. He spoke to her sweetly as he tucked her tiny arms and legs inside, making sure her little ears were covered by the hood. And once more, Lovina was impressed with his gentleness toward Autumn.

"There, Itty-Bit. We don't want you to get cold on the long drive to church," he said.

Gazing up at him, the baby wriggled in response. When he had the child wrapped in a warm blanket for good measure, he picked her up and glanced at Lovina. "Do we have plenty of bottles and goat's milk to last through the day for her?"

Lovina nodded and jutted her chin toward

the diaper bag. "*Ja*, I've already put that and plenty of extra nappies in her bag."

"*Gut*! We're ready to go." Jonah clasped the bag and headed for the door. At the last moment, he flipped a corner of the blanket over the baby's face to shield her from the crisp air.

Dawdi took Lovina's arm. "Let me help you. I know what it's like to have pain. I deal with it every day. We can be invalids together."

He chuckled as he helped her shuffle toward the door. He was limping almost as much as her, and she sympathized with the elderly man. It was bad enough to be in discomfort for a day or two because of an injury. She didn't know what she'd do if she had to cope with this all the time.

"I suppose this is a case of the lame helping the lame to walk," Lovina quipped.

Dawdi laughed. "We can only do the best we can do. No more, no less. But at least we can do it together."

Together. She liked that. And for a moment, she wished this man was her real grandpa.

They stepped out onto the porch. Jonah held the door for them, seeming to have no trouble as he juggled the baby and diaper bag with ease.

After securing the door, he accompanied

them to the horse and buggy waiting in the driveway. It seemed Jonah had everything ready and in control. A capable man.

As they walked, Lovina saw puffs of their frozen breath on the frigid air. She noticed the snow had been cleared away from the porch and walk paths.

"Do I have you to thank for shoveling the snow for me today?" she asked Jonah.

He merely looked away and opened the door to the buggy.

"*Ja*, Jonah did it," *Dawdi* supplied. "He wanted to make sure you and the *boppli* were taken care of."

Hmm. Just following the bishop's orders again, no doubt.

"How kind," Lovina said, trying to have a humble heart filled with gratitude.

"It's nothing. You'd do the same for someone in need," Jonah said.

Yes, she would certainly try. It was their way. The Lord had taught them to love one another, no matter what. But as she slid into the back seat of the buggy, she looked at him. Their gazes locked briefly and he handed her the baby. Then he turned away and helped his grandfather. The two men sat in front and within moments, the buggy jerked and they were on their way.

As expected, they arrived late, just after the meeting started. Ever solicitous, Jonah helped Lovina to her seat among the women, then joined *Dawdi* with the other men. Everyone in the congregation turned to look and Lovina's cheeks flamed hot as road flares. They sat on backless wooden benches inside the Burkholders' spacious barn. An old black stove piped out heat from the fire. With approximately eighty occupants, the large room was soon toasty warm.

People glanced at Lovina and the baby, but they didn't look surprised. No doubt, Bishop Yoder had already told most of them she was tending to Autumn until her mother could return. It worked that way among the Amish. Word spread like wildfire. They all knew each other's business, which was both bad and good. They had few secrets, but they could always rely on one another for help.

The preacher's exhortations to love one another as yourself touched Lovina's heart and she chastised herself for feeling grouchy today. The long, drawn-out hymns sung a cappella soothed her nerves. The meeting lasted several hours and the time allowed her ankle to rest. Midway through, she stood to go change Autumn's diaper. It was difficult to carry the baby and hobble with the cane as she tried to take Autumn into a private area where she could care for her. Sarah Yoder, the bishop's wife, was right there to help without saying a word.

Soon it was time to set out lunch for the men and children. Lovina wasn't much help. She sat and fed the baby, feeling absolutely lazy and useless. To make matters worse, in all the confusion, she'd forgotten to bring the two pumpkin pies she'd made for the event. Which meant she had nothing to contribute to the meal.

"I'm so sorry you hurt your ankle. I brought you some lunch." Sarah held out a plate filled with a thick slice of homemade bread spread with peanut butter and marshmallow, a thick wedge of ham, beets, pickles, and cheese.

Though she felt miserable, Lovina pasted a bright smile on her face and accepted the offering with thanks. "*Danke*, that's so kind of you. I really appreciate your help today."

Jonah approached and reached for the baby. "Can I tend to her for a while?"

Looking up into his dark eyes, Lovina saw no censure there. Only an earnest desire to help. Nodding her head, she handed Autumn over. As he walked away, Lovina soon found herself surrounded by women asking after her welfare.

"The bishop told us you were caring for a *boppli* until her *mudder* is feeling better," Rebecca King said.

"That's so kind of you," Sarah said.

Lovina merely nodded. As the bishop's wife, Sarah probably knew the entire story, but since she wasn't sure, Lovina thought it best to say as little as possible.

"*Ach*, look at that. Aren't they cute together?" Hannah Schwartz pointed at Jonah.

In unison, they all lifted their heads and stared at the man. He sat at the long tables with the other men, holding Autumn with one hand while he ate his noon meal with the other.

"He's a natural with children, don't you think?" Norma Albrecht stood just behind Lovina, cradling her own newborn son in her arms.

"I think he is. Look how easily he tends to that *boppli*. He'll make a *gut* husband and *vadder* one day," Sarah said.

Unaware that he was the topic of discussion, Jonah bit into a ham sandwich, seeming deep in conversation with Jeremiah Beiler and Darrin Albrecht, their deacon. The baby promptly spit up on Jonah's pristine shirt. Without missing a beat, he laid his sandwich down, picked up a burp cloth and wiped the milky spittle away. He laughed at something Darrin said. He actually laughed! Lovina stared at the sight, not knowing what to think.

"It's indecent for a man and woman to live together when they're not married," old Marva Geingerich said.

The women stared at her. At the age of ninety-one, she was the matriarch of their congregation. Since she was an Old Order Swartzentruber Amish from Ohio, she disapproved of almost everyone and everything. Prim and proper, she wasn't shy about voicing her opinion.

"But Lovina doesn't live with Jonah," Sarah objected. "He lives out back in the *dawdi haus* with his grandfather."

"Hmph! Close enough. It's not proper, if you ask me," Marva said.

Uncertainly washed over Lovina. She hated to be the topic of gossip but couldn't really do anything about it at this point. As the women looked at her, she saw the suspicion in their eyes. Lovina tried to ignore it and focused on consuming her food. But she had little appetite and thought perhaps she should have stayed home after all.

She tried her hardest not to look at Jonah but her gaze kept drifting back to him. She tried to tell herself it was so she could check on Autumn. But deep in her heart, she knew it was something more. Something she didn't understand.

Yes, Jonah did seem comfortable with the baby, considering he wasn't married and had no children of his own. But Lovina sensed something in Norma's and Sarah's words. She'd seen this happen time and time again. Women in her *Gmay* would frequently point out the attractive attributes of some eligible bachelor, hoping to push them into marriage. But it wouldn't work with her. At the advanced age of twenty-six, Lovina was determined to remain an independent old maid.

Instead of taking their bait, she turned toward Norma so she didn't have to look at Jonah and his handsome, smiling face.

"How are you feeling this week? It can take time for your body to recover after having a *boppli*. Is the fatigue easier now?" she asked the new mother.

Having successfully changed the topic, she was grateful to be discussing something other than Jonah or Autumn. But throughout the day, her gaze kept straying to Jonah and the baby. And for one brief moment, she let herself imagine that they belonged to her and they were a happy *familye* attending church. But that wasn't her life. It wasn't her truth. And she'd do better to remain grounded in reality.

The women were watching him again. Jonah felt it without even looking up. They laughed and he shifted Autumn's weight in his arms, feeling nervous and self-conscious. No doubt Lovina and the other women were discussing him. And as he wondered what they were saying, he didn't like being their hot topic. Not one bit.

"Can I hold her?"

He looked up and found Fannie and her husband, Alvin, standing beside him. Lunch was winding down and he scooted back his chair as he stood. A fissure of nerves pulsed over him. Since their engagement had ended, he'd avoided Fannie like the plague. She'd done the same and he wondered why she'd approached him now.

"Of course." He handed the baby over, looping his thumbs through his suspenders while she cuddled the child against her throat.

Pressing her face close to Autumn's chubby cheeks, Fannie released a chuckle. She inhaled deeply, as if breathing the baby in. "*Ach*, she smells so sweet."

"Um, that's Lovina's doing. She has this special lotion she rubs on the *boppli* every day after her bath," Jonah said.

Fannie laughed again, a shrill, girlish snicker that made Jonah cringe.

Funny. Her laugh never grated on him before. But it did now. And he wondered why.

She didn't seem to hear him as she tilted a shy, sidelong look at her husband. In response, Alvin wrapped one arm around her shoulders. Jonah caught a look of devotion in the man's eyes. A sear of pain burned Jonah's heart as he stepped back, feeling like an intruder. Fannie wasn't his fiancée anymore. She was another man's wife. But then Jonah overheard Alvin whisper words that pierced him to the core.

"Just think. In seven months, we'll be holding our own *boppli*. It won't be long now," he said.

Fannie nodded and released another set of girlish giggles.

Jonah turned away, blinking at the intensity of emotion burning through his veins. Fannie was pregnant! With Alvin's child! It was to be expected. After all, they'd married five months earlier. But it still hurt Jonah.

And that's when a thought occurred to him. This couple was truly in love. Fannie hadn't loved Jonah. Not the way a woman should love a man. Not for richer and poorer, for better or worse. And maybe Jonah had never really loved her, either. But their breakup had stung his pride, something he didn't like to admit. The Lord taught that he should be humble and shun pride. But that was easier said than done. And in that moment, Jonah couldn't help comparing Lovina's calm maturity with Fannie's silly outbursts. It took a lot for him to admit to himself that Lovina was right. He never would have been fully happy with Fannie. Maybe their breakup had been for the best. But her rejection—one of many he'd experienced over his lifetime—cut him deep. He'd been hurt too many times to ever let his guard down again.

"Jonah, would you join Lovina and me for a moment?"

He looked up and saw Bishop Yoder beckoning to him.

"I'll watch the *boppli* for you," Fannie said.

Grateful for the distraction, Jonah nodded and crossed the barn to where Lovina sat waiting. The bishop quickly led them to a corner where they could have a moment of privacy. Lovina used her cane to hobble along. Seeing her awkward movements, Jonah quickly pulled up a chair for her.

"Sit and rest yourself," he said.

Nodding her thanks, Lovina sat.

"I just wanted to update you two," the bishop began. "I've sent letters to all the bishops in the area and am waiting for a response. You haven't heard anything, have you?"

They shook their heads, then he frowned.

"If we can't find Autumn's *mamm*, we'll need to place her in a permanent Amish home with both a *mudder* and a *vadder*," he said.

Lovina's delicate eyebrows drew downward and she released a gasp of dismay. "So soon? When are you planning to do that?"

Bishop Yoder held up a hand to reassure her. "Not yet. We've got time. Thanksgiving is coming soon and may delay things for a while. I'll wait until I hear from all the bishops before I make any changes, so rest at ease."

The bishop's words upset Lovina. Jonah could tell by the way she twined her hands nervously in her lap. He looked away, focusing on what the bishop was saying, trying to ignore Lovina and her beautiful blue eyes. Because he was not interested in her or any woman. He told himself he didn't care what she was thinking. He didn't care that she was hurting over the thought of giving up little

Autumn. But he knew that was a lie. Because the idea upset him, too.

The bishop talked with them several more minutes, asking about the baby's health and how she was sleeping. From everything Jonah had seen, Lovina took excellent care of the child, even when she'd sprained her own ankle. Finally the bishop left to speak with other members of their congregation. Lovina sat there, staring at her hands. Silent as a stone.

"Geht es dir gut?" Jonah asked after her welfare.

Lovina looked up at him, her eyes sparkling with tears. *"Ja,* I'm fine. But Jonah, I don't know what I'll do if the bishop takes Autumn and gives her to someone else. I love her so much. She deserves to have caring parents raise her. And the thought of losing her to strangers… It would be like giving up my son all over again. I just don't think I can stand it."

She bit her bottom lip and looked away, as if she realized she'd said too much. She quickly wiped her eyes with the backs of her hands. "I'm sorry. I… I shouldn't have said all that."

No, she shouldn't have. Because it reminded Jonah that Lovina had given away her own child, just like his mother had walked away from him. And her regrets didn't soften his heart toward her. She'd made her choice. The fact that she felt bad about it now was a little late for her child.

He stood there like a great lump of coal, not knowing what to say. He hadn't expected her confession at all. Her words surprised him, especially since he loved Autumn, too. He hated to lose the baby when he'd grown so attached to her. A part of him hoped the bishop never found her mother. But the tenets of his faith dictated that he must be married in order to keep the baby. And that was not something he was prepared to do. Not now, not ever. Autumn could not stay with him and Lovina indefinitely. He knew that. Okay, fine! But it would break his heart once more when Bishop Yoder finally took the baby away.

"The bishop is trying to do what's best for Autumn," he said. "He won't give her to just anyone. She'll be loved by her new *familye*. Everything will work out fine. We have to believe that and put our faith in *Gott*."

Jonah didn't know why he bothered to re-assure Lovina. Maybe he said the words out loud because he needed to hear them, too. But when she looked up at him, her eyes so wide and filled with doubt, he found himself longing to wrap his arms around her and kiss her tears away. A totally ridiculous idea if ever he'd heard one.

"Do you really think so?" she asked, her voice a trembling whisper.

"*Ja*, I know so," he said, forcing himself to believe it.

She nodded and showed a sad little smile. She looked so forlorn that it was on the tip of his tongue to say something kind. Something to buoy her spirits. But he knew that would only bond them closer. And right now, he wasn't prepared to take the risk. His heart couldn't stand it. So before he could speak, he clenched his teeth, turned and walked away.

Chapter Seven

Lovina stared after Jonah. Surrounded by members of her church congregation, people laughing, eating and chatting all around her, she'd never felt more alone in her life. What on earth had possessed her to divulge those things to Jonah? She felt stupid and foolish. Of all the people to confide in, he was the last person who cared what she thought. And yet she'd opened a teensy corner of her heart and told him things she'd barely admitted to herself.

For years, she'd worked hard. To never let down her guard. To build an independent life where she didn't need anyone else. And it worked…for a while. She hadn't been hurt in a long, long time. But then little Autumn had fallen into her life. And now she'd cried and blabbed her innermost thoughts to a man who didn't approve of her. Yet she felt so comfortable with Jonah. Too comfortable. She'd grown overly accustomed to being near him.

Oh, no! The awful truth reared its ugly head. She'd come to rely on him. To anticipate his morning visits and even enjoy working with him.

Well, that was the end of it. Something hardened inside her. She must pull back and keep her thoughts and needs to herself. The bishop had asked Jonah to look out for her and Autumn. To keep them safe. But Lovina didn't need Jonah or anyone. And she certainly should not have told him her innermost feelings. She must not ask him for help ever again. Sprained ankle or not, she would rely on herself and no one else. But when the time came, how could she face losing Autumn? She was so attached to the baby. One day, she knew she'd have to let go. Eventually, the bishop would take Autumn away. Lovina tried to tell herself once the bishop found Autumn's mother, the baby would go home and be happy. Everything would return to normal.

Or would it?

An hour later, Autumn was back in Lovina's arms as Jonah assisted the men in cleaning up the barn. He helped stack the benches and tables in the church wagon—a large black enclosed wagon with a red "slow-moving vehicle" triangle on the back. It would be driven over to the Hostetlers' farm so they could host church in two weeks. And from the looks of things, Jonah and the men were almost finished with their chore.

Lovina rocked Autumn in her arms, gazing at the sleeping baby's delicate features. Memories washed over her as she thought about her own little boy and the few times she'd been able to hold him like this. Daggers of regret and guilt pierced her heart. She often thought of returning to Pennsylvania where she had aunts and uncles and cousins. But she couldn't go back. Not after what she'd done. They all knew her shame. And her child's father was living there still. She'd had a letter from her great-aunt several years earlier. He'd married some cute Amish girl and now had a passel of kids. She could never live there again and see him regularly at church and their other gatherings. He'd moved on, so why couldn't she? She must press forward. She was absolutely certain it was what the Lord wanted her to do. And yet she couldn't seem to.

"Lovina, are you ready to go *heemet* now?"

She jerked and glanced up. *Dawdi* Noah stood several feet away, leaning heavily on his cane. His kind smile brought her cheer. Over the past few months, he'd become more of a father to her than her own dad. Without waiting for her answer, he reached down and picked up the diaper bag.

"*Ja*, I'm ready when you and Jonah are," Lovina said.

Dawdi turned, lost his footing, dropped the bag and reached out to brace a hand against the wall before he fell. Lovina jumped up and would have hurried over to help him but he held out a hand to stop her.

"I'm *allrecht*!" he insisted.

Lovina wasn't so sure. His cheeks were bright red and his breathing heavy from his exertions. Cradling the baby with one arm, she ignored his rebuttal and pulled a stool over for him to rest on.

"Here. Sit a moment. Jonah doesn't look like he's quite ready yet," she said.

Dawdi's bushy eyebrows twitched as he slid onto a chair. "Have you had a nice day, or has it been difficult for you?"

She looked down, fingering the smooth edge of Autumn's fleece bundling bag. "It's been okay. I haven't done a single thing to help the women. People have been kind, and Jonah has tended to Autumn most of the afternoon. I feel lazy but my ankle isn't hurting now. And the *boppli* has been *gut* as gold."

They both gazed at the baby. She looked so innocent and sweet, completely reliant upon their care. She had no idea how precarious her situation was.

"*Ach*, the poor *kind*," *Dawdi* said.

Thinking he was referring to the baby, Lovina nodded in understanding. "I know. But don't worry. We'll take *gut* care of little Autumn."

He whipped his head up and his eyebrows lowered in confusion. "Of course you will. But I was speaking about her *mudder*."

"Oh." Bewilderment fogged Lovina's mind but she liked that *Dawdi* felt compassion for the young woman. For whatever reasons, she'd felt desperate enough to give her baby to strangers.

"She must feel completely alone. Why else would she give her *boppli* to you?" *Dawdi* asked, as if reading her mind.

It touched her heart that *Dawdi* seemed to understand. She longed to confide her inner feelings about marriage to him but wasn't sure she dared trust him. Not with something so personal.

"I don't know what her situation is but I hope she somehow finds her way," Lovina said.

Dawdi pursed his lips together and nodded in agreement. "*Ja*, we mustn't judge. The poor *maedel*. She must be so frightened to give away her *boppli* like this."

That was true. Maybe *Dawdi* grasped more than she realized.

"It's possible her *familye* doesn't even know she had a *boppli*," he continued. "That's what happened to my *dochder* when she gave birth to Jonah. We didn't know she was expecting and she was afraid to tell us, so she ran away. Then when she went into labor, an *Englisch* midwife brought her home to us. We were shocked but tried to figure everything out. She left three days later in the middle of the night. All she left us was Jonah and a note saying she didn't want to be Amish anymore. We searched for her but never heard from her again."

Really? Lovina hadn't known that. And how did that make Jonah feel? She couldn't help but wonder.

"Perhaps Autumn's *mudder* kept her pregnancy a secret, too," she said.

That's what Lovina had done. No one knew,

except her boyfriend. It was winter and easy for her to hide her condition.

Dawdi reached out and patted her hand, his palm calloused from years of hard work. "It must have been difficult for her. And for you."

Lovina blinked. It was no secret when Lovina moved to Colorado that she'd had a child out of wedlock. Before he'd left their faith and divorced her mother, Lovina's dad had told almost everyone in their *Gmay* about her pregnancy. Because of the tenets of their faith, her mom could never remarry as long as her father was alive, because it would be considered adultery. It wasn't something Lovina was proud of. But *Dawdi* and Jonah were newer to their community. She could only wonder who told them about her past.

"*Ja*, it was very hard," she said, unwilling to talk about it more than that. It was too embarrassing. Too painful. And she'd already confided way too much to Jonah.

Yes, she'd kept her pregnancy secret. But in the end, when she'd finally confessed to her father that she was expecting a child, he'd been furious. He'd promptly sent her to Kansas to live with strangers until her baby was born a month later. After the birth, she'd had two glorious days alone with her little boy…

until her dad showed up and stole the baby away like a thief in the night. Now she wondered if Autumn's mother had faced a similar situation at home.

"Jonah's still angry at his *mudder* for leaving him all those years ago," *Dawdi* said.

Lovina heard the pain and regret in the elderly man's voice. She squeezed his hand tight, offering silent support. In all honesty, she was surprised he was confiding so much to her. But the two of them seemed to have a connection.

"I'm sorry, *Dawdi*. I know it must have been difficult for you. I... I was only fourteen when I found myself in a similar situation. I just wish I could go back in time and change the outcome. I wish I could have raised my son."

He showed a slight smile. "Fourteen is awful young to try to raise a child. There's nothing for you to be sorry about in giving him up."

"That's just it! I didn't give him up. My *vadder* took him from me." She blurted the words before she could stop them. Her voice and hands trembled. It brought her a lot of shame to speak badly about her father. With her upbringing among the Amish, it wasn't appropriate, and she clamped her mouth shut. She'd said enough already.

Dawdi gazed at her for several pounding moments. "I'm sorry for that. You're a *gut* woman, no one can deny that. No doubt your *vadder* thought he was doing what was right for you and your *boppli*."

Lovina doubted it. Looking back, she thought her father was one of the most self-serving men she'd ever met. And if she saw him today, she'd give him an earful. No matter what, she still felt culpable. At least for her own errors. Her greatest fear was that her own son might grow up like Jonah, believing she'd abandoned him. And she hadn't! But she could do nothing about it now. Instead, she put her trust in *Gott* and prayed He cared for her little boy all the days of his life. She prayed he felt happy and loved by his parents.

"Jonah is a kindhearted man, too. He'll find his way," she said, hoping it was true.

Dawdi shrugged and breathed a sad little sigh. "He is kind, but I think he's been hurt too many times. He has difficulty with trust. He doesn't let down his guard easily. I worry about him, especially since Autumn has *komm* to live with us. I see how it eats him up inside. The anguish and pain. He never knew his *mudder*. And none of us know who his *vadder* was. An *Englischer*, that's all we know. But I don't think Jonah can ever be truly happy until he's able to forgive his *mamm* for leaving him."

That made Lovina sad. What if her son felt the same? She hated the thought that he'd go through life resenting her for something she hadn't wanted. She couldn't stand to think about it and purposefully pushed it aside. She must have faith the Lord would make it all right one day.

They sat in silence for several minutes. Lovina didn't know what else to say. No wonder Jonah seemed to dislike her so much. *Dawdi*'s words confirmed her suspicion. Jonah probably thought she'd abandoned her baby. But what good would it do to tell him differently? He was still angry at his own mother. And though he didn't know Lovina's full story, she had no doubt he harbored resentment toward her, too. She tried to tell herself she didn't care but it still bothered her. A lot!

Poor Jonah. He'd grown up not knowing his own mother. And then Fannie had broken off their engagement. Gaining perspective into his past made Lovina wish she could help him somehow. But if she tried, he'd resent her even more. It wasn't her business anyway. She must protect her own heart. She couldn't get involved with Jonah any more than she already was. But that didn't stop her from feeling sympathetic toward him.

Finally, they were on their way home. Jonah released a silent sigh, grateful they'd made it through the day. He sat in the front seat of the buggy with *Dawdi* beside him in the passenger seat. Lovina rode in back with Autumn. The little girl fussed as Lovina made a bottle. Within moments, the baby's loud sucking sounds could be heard and Jonah hid a smile. It seemed odd that this child wasn't of his making, yet she'd wormed her way into his heart anyway. From what Lovina said, she felt the same. Though caring for the child wasn't a permanent arrangement, Jonah didn't want to give her up any more than Lovina did. They both loved Autumn, which seemed strange and personal since it was something they shared with no one else.

They were all quiet, lost in their own thoughts. Night was coming, cold and dark, with just a bit of moonlight gleaming in the sky to show the way. Jonah flipped on the battery-operated headlights, peering through the blackness as he turned onto the county road. They'd lingered too long at church, catching up on everyone's lives and tidying up the barn after service. If Lovina hadn't hurt her ankle, he knew she'd have been in the kitchen, washing dishes with the other women. It was their way. To help one another all they could.

Most of the men and women in their congregation were kind to Jonah and *Dawdi*. The Amish were just like any other people. In spite of their religious beliefs, some were harsher and more judgmental than others. But after four years, Jonah and his father were part of the group. Aside from the constant matchmaking, Jonah liked this *Gmay*. And for the first time since he'd decided to move back east, he realized it would be difficult to leave this area when the time came. Even though his farm was too small, he tried to tell himself he didn't want to leave because he'd put so much work into the place. But now he wondered if that was the only reason he thought about staying.

Jonah slapped the leads against the horse, spurring him into a faster trot. The black pavement loomed before them. At least it was clear of ice. Even with the lights on the buggy, Jonah didn't feel safe. Too many trucks and cars zipped along the road at a frantic pace, and it wasn't secure for them to be out so late.

"Nice news about Fannie and Alvin, don't

you think?" *Dawdi* broke the silence, speaking in a cheery tone.

Out of his peripheral vision, Jonah caught the movement of Lovina sitting forward a bit.

"*Ja*, it's tremendous news. She asked if I'd be her midwife," she said.

"When is her *boppli* due?" *Dawdi* asked.

"In the spring."

Jonah kept silent, listening to every word. In his mind, he still couldn't help thinking Fannie should have been his wife. This should be his baby. And they weren't.

In the faded light, Lovina looked at Jonah, as if assessing his mood.

"What do you think about the news, Jonah?" *Dawdi* asked.

Jonah paused, taking a deep breath and letting it go before he spoke. "I think it's to be expected. Fannie and Alvin are married. They're bound to have *kinder*."

Both *Dawdi* and Lovina stared at him through the shadows, as if disappointed in his answer. And during the lull in conversation, he took a moment to ask himself what he thought. Honestly, he felt torn. On the one hand, he was delighted for them. But on the other hand, it ripped his heart to shreds.

"I think it's *wundervoll* news. I'm happy for them," he finally said.

Yes, he was genuinely pleased for Fannie. Anything else would be uncharitable. Though she'd broken his heart, he was glad she was in love. Glad she'd found happiness and peace. Her husband seemed to actually care for her. Her childlike manners didn't seem to bother Alvin. And she seemed much calmer and happier with him than she'd been with Jonah. Maybe Lovina was right...he and Fannie weren't well suited. Maybe he'd dodged a bad marriage after all. But that didn't change his mind about moving back east. *Dawdi* just wanted Jonah to be happy and would do whatever he liked. It was bad enough seeing Fannie share her good news with everyone in their congregation. He couldn't stand the thought of sticking around to watch her raise a passel of kids while he remained single. He still wanted out of here as fast as he could go.

He glanced at his grandfather, who stared at him without flinching.

"What?" Jonah said, wondering what the old man expected.

"Are you sure you're okay with it?" *Dawdi* asked.

Jonah looked away, focusing on the road. He shrugged, trying to keep the resentment from filling his voice. "I don't really have a choice, do I? I certainly don't want to be married to a woman who doesn't love me. I told you, I'm better off being alone the rest of my life."

"*Ach*, you're better off being married to a woman who loves you, but you're not better off being single. It's time you found someone else to wed. We have many eligible young women in our *Gmay*. You need to look harder," *Dawdi* said.

In the rearview mirror, he saw that Lovina was overly quiet, listening to this exchange, her eyes bright and wide. And though she was always around lately, Jonah reminded himself she wasn't part of his *familye*. She didn't belong in this moment. Not when he was discussing something so private with his grandfather.

"I don't want to talk about it right now, *Dawdi*. Marriage isn't for everyone. Not all of us find that special someone we want to grow old with." Jonah spoke low.

Lovina sat back on the padded seat with a little bump. In the quiet that followed, Jonah was almost certain he heard her mumble under her breath.

"I agree with you there."

He tilted his head toward her. "Did you say something, Lovina?"

"Nothing of importance," she said.

Maybe not but he knew he'd heard her correctly. And her words startled him. Did Lovina prefer being single, too? By Amish standards, she was definitely considered an old maid. But why didn't she want to marry? He'd never thought about it before. Was she still single because she preferred it that way? Or because she'd had her heart broken like him? It didn't make sense. She was a beautiful, proficient woman who would make any Amish man an ideal wife. And yet she'd never married.

Why?

The even clip-clop of the horse's hooves filled the air. *Dawdi* released a sigh and leaned his head back against the seat. After a few moments, Jonah thought he'd fallen asleep.

He was wrong.

"After church services, I saw the two of you talking with the bishop," *Dawdi* said. "Did he have any news about Autumn's *mudder*?"

Jonah paused, purposefully letting Lovina respond.

"*Ne*, nothing new to report. He wondered if we'd heard anything, too. He mailed off the letters to all the bishops in the area quite some time ago but no one has responded back. I guess we're waiting to hear," she said.

Dawdi sat up straighter. "But what happens if none of them know who the *mudder* is?"

"He said he knows a *gut* couple who can raise Autumn as their own," Lovina said.

Jonah turned in her direction. He caught the note of anxiousness in her voice.

"Autumn's *mudder* may not be from around here," Jonah said. "She may be from another state. The Amish talk and word spreads. Someone may have told her about our midwife. But for her to abandon her own child the way she did, we may never find her. It's what she wanted, after all. To dump her responsibility on Lovina and be left alone."

That old feeling of resentment surged inside Jonah. He tried not to sound condemning or unkind but it didn't quite come out like that.

"You're being judgmental again," Lovina pointed out in a rather tart tone. "We don't know what Autumn's *mamm* is going through or what her motivations are. From the note she left us, she wants only the best for her *boppli*. And it's not becoming of you to be so unkind."

Jonah gripped the lead lines harder. Lovina had just put him in his place. She had a way of making him feel small and unfair. And yet she was right.

"I'm sorry," he said.

And though he meant it, he still couldn't help feeling angry at Autumn's mother just as he felt angry at his own mom.

They rode in silence the remaining miles to his farm. And when they arrived, he hopped out and helped Lovina gather up the diaper bag and escorted her inside with Autumn.

He switched on the gas-powered light in the kitchen, then turned. As Lovina limped across the room, he noticed the weary slump of her shoulders. She was tired and probably in pain. Yet her own needs were forgotten as she spoke to Autumn in a soothing, sweet voice while she removed the babe from the warm bundling.

A surge of compassion rose within him. What call did he have to be so critical of others when he had so many failings of his own? The Lord asked that he forgive all men and women. That he not judge. And yet that's exactly what he'd done since he'd become aware that his mom had left him behind.

"Is there anything else I can do for you?" he asked.

Lovina shook her head, placing the used bottles in the sink for washing. "*Ne*, we're going up to bed now. Since she's having a *boppli*, I'll need to pay a prenatal visit to Fannie tomorrow."

He didn't say anything for several moments. The last thing he wanted was to drive Lovina over to his ex-fiancée's house. But like Lovina, he would do his duty.

"What time do you want to leave?" he asked.

She turned and faced him, and he saw the fatigue in her eyes along with a strong sense of responsibility. After all, she knew the bishop wanted him to accompany her on her rounds. "I'd like to leave around ten o'clock, if that works for you. The visit shouldn't take long. You don't need to come inside the house, unless you want to."

Hmm. She was making this easier on him. And why didn't that surprise him? Lovina was always so kind. So in tune with what other people were feeling.

"*Allrecht.* I'll be ready with the buggy by then." He turned and stepped outside on the porch.

"*Gut nacht,*" she said, closing the back door firmly behind him.

He stood there for several moments, his fingers cold inside his leather gloves, his breath a puff of steam on the frigid night air. So much had happened at church today, and yet nothing out of the ordinary. But as he walked toward the barn, he didn't feel very good about himself. He knew he needed to forgive and forget. To love others. He must figure out a way to let go of the anguish that filled him every time he thought about his mother and Fannie. He just wasn't sure how to go about it.

Chapter Eight

"Congratulations! I believe you're about ten weeks along," Lovina said.

She sat at a small table in Fannie Fisher's bedroom. Picking up a pen, she jotted several notes on the chart she'd just created for the new mother-to-be. Late-morning sunlight gleamed through the window as Fannie sat at the foot of the bed. She waited as Alvin knelt in front of her and tied the laces to her practical black shoes. Finished with the chore, Alvin stood and stared at his wife with doe-eyed fondness. Lovina looked away.

"Everything is okay, then?" he asked quietly.

Lovina knew his question was for her, though his gaze remained fixed on Fannie. He'd been here while they'd listened to the baby's heartbeat for the first time. It had been a happy experience, to say the least. The couple was practically glowing, filled with the warmth that only new parenthood could bring.

Lovina set her pen down and nodded. "Both *mudder* and *boppli* appear to be just fine."

"You're absolutely sure the *boppli* is *allrecht*?" Fannie asked, smoothing her hands over her long skirts as she stood.

"As far as I can tell, everything looks great. The *boppli*'s heartbeat is strong and appears normal," Lovina said.

She quickly labeled and stowed the vials of blood and urine she'd taken from Fannie in her medical bag. They'd be sent to a lab to check for Rh factor, blood type, anemia, sugar, protein and any possible infections.

"And what about me? Am I okay?" Fannie asked.

Lovina glanced at the young woman, wondering what she meant. Then Lovina noticed a hint of fear in the young woman's eyes.

"*Ach*, sure! Your blood pressure is right where it should be. Once I get the results back from your labs, I'll know more. But I see nothing that alarms me. Nothing at all," she said.

"But my *mamm* had an awful time birthing her six *bopplin*. And I'm built narrow, just like her." Fannie's voice trembled and she clutched Alvin's hand until her knuckles whitened.

Feeling confused, Lovina glanced at the young woman and saw how her forehead creased with worry, her eyes wide and uncertain. She looked almost terrified. In all her years as a midwife, Lovina had never encountered so much anxiety in a new mother. Fannie seemed to need extra reassurance.

Stepping over to the girl, Lovina reached out and squeezed her arm. "Don't fret, Fannie. From your exam, I don't think you'll have trouble giving birth. I believe you'll do just fine. Try to enjoy this experience. Think about your *boppli* and have fun with this special time in your life!"

Fannie blinked at her for several moments, as if she didn't understand. Then she nodded. "*Allrecht*, I'll try."

Inwardly, Lovina took a deep, relaxing breath. Motherhood could be a bit unsettling, especially with the first baby. As Fannie's midwife, Lovina was in this for the long haul and determined to make it as joyful and easy as possible for the new mother.

Lovina met Fannie's gaze without flinching. "Just remember to eat right, take a brisk walk every day and focus on your *boppli*. If you have any concerns whatsoever, no matter how small, you contact me right away. Alvin and I are both here for you."

She glanced at Alvin, who nodded with deep sincerity and stepped even closer to his wife, if that was possible. Lovina tried to sound as upbeat and positive as she could. But in her heart of hearts, she wondered what had induced Jonah to propose to this girl. Fannie was so different from him. The complete opposite. Jonah seemed so solid and down-to-earth whereas Fannie was a huge worrywart. Alvin was more suited to her. He seemed to relish doting on her. Anyone who looked at the couple could tell they were in love. And even when Jonah had been engaged to the girl, Lovina had never seen that kind of devotion between them. If only he could realize their breakup was for the best, he might feel happier.

Lovina packed her fetal Doppler, pregnancy wheel to determine a due date, blood pressure cuff and stethoscope into her medical bag. She noticed Alvin retrieved a clean hanky for his wife to blow her nose, then poured some water for her from a pitcher beside the bed. As he handed her the glass, he spoke gentle words of comfort. Lovina couldn't imagine Jonah fussing over Fannie like this. And yet when she thought about it, Lovina realized Jonah had his own way of caring. Whenever she needed wood for the cookstove, she found the bucket in her kitchen always filled. And since baby Autumn had come to stay with them, Jonah tended to the little girl like any father. He frequently fed and milked Lovina's goats while *Dawdi* gathered the eggs. Of course, Lovina wouldn't call that doting on her, but they were her chores. And though the bishop had assigned Jonah to look after her and the baby, Lovina liked to pretend he did it because he wanted to and not because he felt compelled.

"I'll want to see you again in four weeks," Lovina said as she shrugged into her warm shawl and picked up her bag.

"*Allrecht*. I'll *komm* to your place next time," Fannie said.

"That would be great." It would save Lovina a long trip.

She had no idea if Autumn would still be living with her then. It was easier to tend to the baby in her own house. Right now, Jonah was home with little Autumn…that was the only way he would agree to let Lovina drive herself over here to Fannie's place. Lovina knew he dreaded this prenatal visit with his ex-fiancée, so this morning she'd asked if she could come alone. Even though he had his own work to do, he'd willingly agreed to watch the baby while she was gone. And though Lovina dearly loved Autumn, it felt nice to get away for a change. On the way home, she was going to make a quick detour to the general store in town to buy supplies. She'd be home by lunchtime and Jonah could return to his farmwork.

Lovina stepped out of the room and headed downstairs. Fannie and Alvin followed.

"*Danke* for coming. I'm so excited. We're really going to have a *boppli* of our own." Fannie smiled as she and Alvin accompanied Lovina outside.

A brisk wind blew from the north and Lovina shivered. "You're so *willkomm*. Now, you go back inside where it's warm. I'll see you soon."

Fannie nodded and turned to go inside. Alvin wrapped his arm around his wife's shoulders and opened the door for her, leaving Lovina to climb into her buggy alone. As she stowed her bag in the back, Lovina glanced at the house one last time. The door was securely closed and she was on her own. Taking the lead lines into her gloved hands, she released the brake and urged the horse forward. As the buggy jostled into motion, it felt good to be by herself for the ride into town. A part of her pretended she was out running errands and her *familye* was waiting for her back at home. How she wished it was real. But it wasn't and she shook the feeling off, focusing on the damp road ahead. Thankfully, it was a warmer day with no black ice.

Within an hour, she'd finished her shopping in town, paid her bill and loaded her purchases into the buggy. As she stood on the boardwalk and lifted the last heavy box, Vance Anderson, one of the three real estate agents in town, reached to help her.

"Here, let me get that for you, Mrs. Lapp. It's too heavy for you." He stashed it in the back, then turned to smile at her with big white teeth.

Mrs. Lapp!

"Thank you," she said. But she didn't correct his error. He was *Englisch*, after all, and probably didn't know the Amish very well.

Dressed in blue jeans and a long wool coat with a red scarf around his neck, Vance slid his hands into his pockets and hunched his shoulders against the cold. A middle-aged man with dark hair and a touch of gray at the temples, he wore a full beard and mustache.

"Fancy meeting you here today. I'll be coming out your way tomorrow. Where would you like me to put the for-sale sign?" he asked.

"For-sale sign?" Lovina tilted her head, feeling confused.

"Yeah, Jonah came to see me two days ago. He's selling your farm. I thought you knew. You're his wife, aren't you?"

She shook her head. "No, I just rent the farmhouse from him. We're not married."

Vance took a step closer. "Ah, so you'll be looking for a new place to live once he sells the place, won't you?"

Lovina didn't know what to say. Feelings of uncertainty, anger and disappointment rose up inside her. She shoved them down, forcing herself to remain calm. Jonah wouldn't sell his farm. Would he?

"I… I think you must have me mistaken for someone else," she said.

Vance frowned. "Jonah Lapp. He lives at 4514 County Road 113. That's the place. I listed it on the market just this morning."

Yes, that was Jonah's address! It was Lovina's address, too. Her mind whirled in a melee of chaos. Jonah wouldn't sell. He loved that place. She could tell from the way he tended his livestock, fields and buildings. It was a small farm but he took meticulous care of it all. And what would he do if he sold it off? Where would he go?

Where would she go?

"I've got some great rentals I can show you," Vance persisted. "Or if you're interested in buying your own home, I can show you a few reasonable options. Great asking prices."

Reaching into his pocket, he whipped out a business card and handed it over. She took it, staring at it in frozen silence.

"Um, I don't think so. But thank you, anyway." She hurried to climb inside the buggy.

As she pulled away from the store, Vance waved farewell. Lovina pasted a smile on her face, urging the horse into a quick trot down Main Street. But inside, she was screaming. It couldn't be true. Could it? Jonah wouldn't put his farm up for sale. Not without telling her. She'd only been renting from him about four months now. Her midwifery business was doing well. She didn't want to move again. Surely Jonah would warn her first. Wouldn't he?

She passed the edge of town, her heart beating like a drum. A surge of panic rose upward in her throat. She loved where she lived. It was the first place that felt like a real home. She could never get such a nice setup for her business somewhere else. But in her heart of hearts, she knew it was more than that. It was Autumn, *Dawdi* and Jonah working together with her that made her feel like she had a real home. For the first time in years, she had folks who depended on her. People who really needed her.

And she needed them.

She blinked, wondering where that thought came from. But there it was, rising in her mind like a summer sunrise. No matter how remote and independent she'd tried to be, she still needed others. She needed to feel loved and wanted. Yet she didn't belong to anyone. Not at Jonah's farmhouse, not anywhere.

As she drove home, she told herself not to fret. Surely Jonah had a reasonable explanation. She sensed he was unhappy. No doubt Fannie had broken his heart. So where did that leave Jonah? Even if he forgave Fannie, it couldn't be easy for him to stand back and witness her wedded bliss with Alvin. But Jonah would get over it. Eventually. He wasn't the first, or the last, to suffer a fractured heart. But she could hardly believe he would leave Riverton and all that he'd worked so hard for. At least, not without giving her fair warning that she needed to find a new place to live. Or would he?

* * *

Jonah twisted the socket wrench hard in order to remove the rolling cutter on his seed planter. It gave way and he took the cutter, careful not to drop the cushings out. The quiet barn smelled of fresh straw he'd just spread in the animal stalls. Earlier, he'd fed Autumn and put her down for a nap. *Dawdi* was inside the farmhouse with her, reclining on the sofa in case she woke up. No doubt he was fast asleep, too. But he'd hear the baby if she woke up and alert Jonah.

It was early afternoon and Lovina should be home soon. To avoid driving over to Fannie and Alvin's place, Jonah agreed to look after Autumn…a much more pleasant chore, he must admit.

When he had the new cutter safely in position, he tightened it down. Reaching for the latch on the seed box, he lifted it off. This planter had come with the farm when he'd bought the place four years earlier. It was ancient and needed to be replaced but so far, he'd kept it going with careful maintenance. Maybe in another year, he'd have enough money to buy a new one.

What was he thinking? He'd be gone next year. He'd sell the place and wouldn't be here for early planting in the spring. Which led him to wonder why he was performing this upkeep now.

As he lifted the seed tube up, he discovered lots of dried dirt inside. Knocking it out with a screwdriver, he coughed at the cloud of dust. What if he couldn't sell his farm? It could take a long time. He might be forced to stay here another year, and he told himself it was best to be prepared.

"Jonah?"

He turned, dropping the screwdriver in the process. It bounced off his boot and hit the dirt floor. Glancing up, he saw Lovina standing inside the double barn doors. She pulled them closed, shutting off the frigid breeze.

"You're back." Bending at the waist, he picked up the hand tool and set it aside.

She came to stand beside him, no more than an arm's reach away. He turned aside, forcing himself not to look at her flushed cheeks. She wore her black traveling bonnet over top of her white prayer *kapp*, her blue eyes sparkling, her nose red from the cold. Absolutely lovely.

"The *boppli* should still be asleep. She was tired after her bottle," he said.

"Can I speak with you, please?" Lovina asked.

Something in her voice caused him to swivel

around. In a rush, he noticed how she lifted her chin a couple inches higher, her lips pressed in a tight, disapproving line.

Oh, no! What was wrong now?

"What is it?" He gestured to a large wooden crate where she could perch and chat in comfort. He sat on a bale of hay, forcing himself to focus on her pretty face.

"I… I just came from town. Vance Anderson stopped me on the street and…"

"And he told you I'm selling the farm," he finished for her. He clenched his eyes closed, wishing he'd told her first.

"*Ja.* He said he'll be out here tomorrow and wanted to know where we want him to put the for-sale sign. Is it true, Jonah?"

He looked at her, seeing the rigid set of her shoulders and the angst in her eyes.

"*Ja*, it's true. I've asked Vance to put the farm on the market," he said.

Her back stiffened. "And when were you going to tell me?"

A flush of regret filled his chest. "Later this evening, once you got *heemet.*"

"But why? Why would you sell your farm?" she asked, her voice filled with incredulity.

"Because there's nothing for me here." The words burst forth before he could stop them.

"Nothing? You have this farm. You have

people who care for you. I wouldn't call that nothing," she said.

Though there was a pleading tone in her words, he thought she was doing an admirable job of maintaining her temper. It was something he admired about her. If this was Fannie, she'd be in hysterics by now. But not Lovina. No, she was always steady and calm. So strong. So reliable.

"I'm sorry, Lovina. You have every right to be upset. But I didn't realize you would feel so strongly about me selling the place. I figured you'd just rent a room from one of our other Amish families in the area. Forgive me for not telling you sooner." He meant every word but his apology seemed rather hollow now.

She looked at him without flinching, without blinking. But in her eyes, he saw a glimmer of moisture. She was near tears and that tore him up inside.

"Of course I forgive you. But what am I supposed to do now?" she asked.

He couldn't answer. He didn't know what to say.

"*Ach*, do you know when you'll sell the place? Have you had any offers?" she asked.

He stood and took two steps toward her even as she stood and took two steps back.

"*Ne,* I have no offers yet. I only just listed the place a couple of days ago. Vance said it could take a long time to sell or no time at all. The market is pretty depressed, so I don't know."

"I'll… I'll have to move again. This is the first place I've felt happy in years and…and now it's being taken from me."

Her voice trembled. Her confession opened a part of her that she'd kept hidden from him until now. A part that told him she was as lonely as him. And that's when he realized she wasn't as strong as she appeared. He opened his mouth to express regret once more but she turned and swept across the expanse of the barn so fast that he felt frozen in place. Without a word or backward glance, she left with a chilling gust of wind, quietly securing the doors behind her.

Jonah sat there and stared after her for quite some time. He thought about running after her. To apologize and plead with her to understand. He had to go. He must! But all at once, the thought of moving away and never seeing her again left him feeling sad and empty inside, and he couldn't for the life of him understand why.

Thanksgiving was just days away, followed by Christmas soon after. But in the frame of mind he was in right now, Jonah couldn't seem to find a lot to feel grateful for. Instead, he felt as though he'd just lost his best friend. A silly notion if ever he'd heard one. Because he and Lovina weren't friends. They couldn't be.

Why hadn't he told her he was selling the farm? The question made his thoughts scatter. He wasn't sure. He should have done so. She deserved that much honesty. After all, she needed time to find another place to live and run her midwifery business. But he hadn't wanted to alarm her. He'd planned to tell her but kept putting it off for some crazy reason. He wasn't sure why. Yet he'd dreaded it. Because as soon as she knew, she would start packing her bags.

Maybe, just maybe, deep down in his heart he was hoping the farm wouldn't sell. But that didn't help him now. Because he had listed the property. He would sell the place and move back east with *Dawdi* and they would start anew.

"Jonah, what did you say to Lovina? She just ran into the house and I think she's upstairs crying."

He looked up and found his grandfather standing just inside the door.

Oh, no! This kept getting worse and worse. Lovina was in tears. And he hated the thought that he'd made her cry. But right now, he didn't want to hear a lecture from his grandpa.

"I told her I'm selling the farm," Jonah said.

Dawdi's bushy gray eyebrows lifted in surprise and he slipped his thumbs through his black suspenders as he came to stand beside Jonah. The old man chewed his bottom lip, as if mulling this over.

"I thought you told her several weeks ago, like you said you were going to do," *Dawdi* said.

"I know, but I put it off. I was going to tell her tonight but she found out from my real estate agent in town."

Dawdi nodded in understanding. "You should have told her, *sohn*."

"I know, I know. But honestly, *Dawdi*, I don't know why she's upset. It's not like this was ever going to be a permanent *heemet* for her. She must have known she would have to find another place eventually."

Heaving a labored sigh, *Dawdi* sat beside him on the bale of hay. "Jonah, everyone has their own grief. Even Lovina. No one is immune to the hardships of life. You know I felt heartbroken when your *mamm* abandoned you as a new *boppli*. She gave up her faith and walked away from her *familye* and everything she'd ever known so she could become *Englisch*."

He said *Englisch* as if it was a dirty word.

"*Ja*, I know. It must have hurt you and *Grossmudder* very much when she left," Jonah conceded.

"It did. For a long time, we thought we must have been horrible parents. We wondered what we'd done wrong. Maybe we didn't teach our *dochder* well enough. Maybe we didn't love her enough. Otherwise, why would she do the things she did?" *Dawdi* asked.

"It wasn't your fault, *Dawdi*. My *mudder* made her own choices," Jonah said.

Dawdi pointed a finger at him and narrowed his eyes with determination. "That's exactly right. You hit the nail on the head. Your *mudder* chose for herself, just as we all must choose."

"You mustn't blame yourself," Jonah insisted.

"I don't. Not anymore. But I still have many regrets," *Dawdi* said. "Everyone has their freedom to choose how they'll live, but our decisions can hurt others. The best we can do is love and serve one another as Jesus Christ taught us to do. It's the greatest commandment of all."

Jonah nodded, feeling guilty for thinking only of himself. Until now, he'd never really thought about how his mother's actions must have hurt his grandparents. "*Ja*, I know that. And I'm sorry for hurting Lovina. I'm grateful you were there to raise me."

Dawdi clapped a hand against Jonah's back with fondness. "It was my pleasure. But remember something. Lovina's *vadder* abandoned her, too. Knowing her the way we do, I don't believe it was easy for her to give up her *boppli*. She told me she was only fourteen years old at the time. Little more than a child herself."

Jonah frowned. This was the first time he'd heard how young she was. "She was only fourteen?"

"*Ja*, very young. We must not be unfair or judgmental toward her. From what I've observed over the past four years that we've known her, Lovina is a pious, hardworking woman with an overly generous heart. We mustn't be unkind to her. Especially when we each have many faults of our own to deal with."

Jonah was very quiet, especially when his grandfather quoted a well-known scripture from the book of Matthew. *Dawdi*'s voice sounded low and quiet but filled with a deep richness that Jonah couldn't deny...like the rushing of many waters.

"Why beholdest thou the mote in thy brother's eye, but consider not the beam that's in thine own eye? First, cast out the beam out of thine own eye and then shalt thou see clearly to cast out the mote out of thy brother's eye."

With those words, *Dawdi* stood and left the barn. Jonah sat there, speechless and ashamed. He'd felt so angry over the wrongs he perceived that had been done against him over the years that he never stopped to realize he was being so critical and harsh of others. And suddenly, he started thinking deeply. It was as if a window opened to his heart. He saw Lovina with a fresh set of eyes. Her rights or wrongs were not for him to judge. Who was he to find fault with someone else when he had so many of his own failings to repent from? But recognizing this didn't change his mind about selling the farm. In fact, it made him even more determined to leave the area as soon as possible. He needed a fresh start somewhere else, far away from his heartache.

Chapter Nine

The week of Thanksgiving, Lovina avoided Jonah like the plague. Not easy to do, considering they lived on the same farm. Though she was able to slip in and out of the barn to milk her goats, he still brought her firewood every morning. But she used the baby as an excuse to not be in the kitchen when he came inside the house. And rather than have him accompany her to visit her expectant mothers, she'd arranged at church for the moms to come to her. That meant very little travel… and a bad case of cabin fever.

Stepping outside on the front porch, she put weight on her injured ankle, testing its strength. It wasn't perfect but it was getting better every day and she could manage without help.

She folded her arms and inhaled the crisp

air as she bid farewell to her last client of the day. It was late afternoon and Autumn was still down for her nap. If Lovina hurried, she might have just enough time to start supper and whip together pumpkin pies for Thanksgiving dinner in a few days.

She glanced at the for-sale sign planted smack-dab in the middle of the front lawn. A constant reminder that she would soon have to leave. So far, no one had come to view the property. A part of her hoped no one would. And yet another part of her wanted Jonah to be happy. And that meant he needed to sell the farm and move away.

Back in the kitchen, she glanced at the local newspaper and rental ads spread across her table. She'd circled several possibilities with a bright red marker. Though she'd mailed off a few inquiries to find a suitable place, nothing appealed to her. She wanted to stay right here.

She reached for a mixing bowl, fighting off a feeling of deep frustration. Who knew how long she had before Jonah sold the place? Thanksgiving was upon them and she felt anything but cheerful. The holidays had always been a source of sadness for her, probably because she had very little *familye* to celebrate with. But this year, she felt even more morose than usual. She reminded herself that Christmas was about the Savior's birth. And because of Him, she was never really alone. But she couldn't help wishing for more.

As she cubed raw carrots and potatoes for a stew, she forced herself to count her many blessings. Maybe she would invite Jonah and *Dawdi* to share Thanksgiving dinner with her. It was logical, after all. She certainly couldn't eat an entire turkey on her own. And she had no doubt the preparation of a big meal was beyond *Dawdi*'s culinary skills. Then again, maybe they had been asked to join one of the many families in their *Gmay*. Since she'd had no such invitation, she could very well find herself spending the day alone, which would be awful.

Within an hour, she had a bubbling pot simmering on her stove, fresh corn bread in the oven and batter for several pumpkin pies ready to pour into the crusts. A thin cry came from the back of the house, and she quickly wiped her hands as she went to get Autumn.

The baby lay on her back, waving her little arms in excitement. She'd kicked her blanket off, but Lovina didn't think the room felt too cold.

Leaning over, Lovina smiled and spoke lovingly as she tried to coax a smile out of the tiny girl. Autumn was almost two months old and it was time to reach this milestone. But in spite of her best efforts, the baby merely gazed at her with sober intensity. No matter. Lovina kissed the girl and continued talking as she changed her diaper.

"You're such a *gut* girl. Are you hungry? I'll get you fed soon enough." She lifted the baby to her shoulder.

In the kitchen, Lovina quickly prepared a bottle and sat in a chair to feed the child. Autumn sucked ravenously, her big blue eyes never wavering from Lovina's face.

As she burped the baby, Lovina heard loud voices coming from outside. She stood, peering out the kitchen window to see what was amiss.

Jonah was hurrying away from the *dawdi haus*, his long legs moving fast as he headed toward the barn. He wore no coat but had on oven mitts as he carried a frying pan that billowed black smoke. *Dawdi* Noah followed on his heels, gesturing wildly and looking miserable as he limped heavily on his wooden cane. Without glancing his way, Jonah doused the sizzling pan in the water barrel.

Oh, dear. It looked like *Dawdi* had burned their supper again.

"I'm sorry, *sohn*. That old stove is just too

hot. I'm afraid it got the better of me," *Dawdi* exclaimed in a rather loud, regretful voice.

Lovina didn't catch Jonah's reply. His words were too soft to overhear. But she saw him turn and remove the oven mitts before he placed a calming hand on his grandfather's shoulder. Even from this distance, Lovina saw his kind gesture as he lifted a hand to placate the elderly man. Rather than yelling at his grandpa, Jonah offered him reassurance. Jonah's mellow empathy impressed Lovina like nothing else could. And in a moment of compassion, she broke her own promise not to invite them in for another meal.

Placing Autumn in her bassinet beside the table, Lovina walked to the back door. She stepped outside onto the porch and lifted a hand to her mouth as she yelled to the two men.

"It looks like you're in need of a hearty supper," she called.

Both men jerked. Jonah whirled around and stared in surprise.

"*Komm* inside and share my meal. I've got plenty of food here," she said.

Dawdi immediately smiled and waved, his expression one of utter relief. Jonah just frowned. For a moment, Lovina thought he might refuse. In a stubborn gesture, she decided it was too cold to stand out here and argue with him. If he wanted to eat, he could come inside. If not, he could suit himself.

Turning, she returned to the kitchen and busied herself with her work. She was facing the gas-powered stove when she heard the creak of the screen door. It clapped closed and the chilly breeze was shut off. Forcing herself not to turn around, she glanced at Autumn. The baby was restless and let out a squall but Lovina didn't pick her up. Instead, she spoke to the girl as she poured the pumpkin mixture into her pie crusts.

"You're *allrecht, liebchen*. Give me a few minutes and I'll get you," she said, reaching for a pot holder.

"I'll tend her," Jonah said.

The clatter of boots on her hardwood floors told her both men had come inside. Still, Lovina ignored them.

"Sit anywhere," she called without looking their way.

Out of the corner of her eye, Lovina saw Jonah step over to pick up the fussy baby. She pulled a pan of steaming corn bread out of the oven and set it aside on the counter to cool. Then she slid the pies in and set a battery-operated timer for forty-five minutes. So the crusts wouldn't get overly brown, she'd covered the edges with tinfoil.

"There, Itty-Bit. I've got you," Jonah spoke low.

Lovina shivered as that old feeling of safety and comfort washed over her. She couldn't understand the impact Jonah's presence had on her. It didn't make sense.

"This is kind of you," *Dawdi* said.

"It's no problem. We'll be ready to eat in just a moment," she said.

She turned and saw Jonah staring at all the papers and classified ads still spread across her table. The heat of awkwardness rushed up her neck and she quickly gathered them and stashed them in the other room. Now that she was being evicted, she didn't want Jonah to know her business.

Jonah cradled Autumn in the crook of his arm as he sat in one of the wooden chairs. Lovina quickly washed, then set the table, noticing how the baby stared up at him with rapt attention. He tilted his head, looking directly into the little girl's eyes as he spoke in that conciliatory voice of his.

"Have you eaten yet, little girl? Or are you starving again, as usual?" he asked.

"I just fed her," Lovina said.

"*Ach*, is that right?" Jonah asked, still gazing at the baby. "So you're trying to fool me into giving you another bottle, is that it?"

In response, the baby smiled. She actually smiled! Lovina stared in shock. At first, she thought she must have imagined it. But no! Jonah had done what she hadn't been able to do. He'd cajoled Autumn to smile.

"*Ach*, you're such a sweet *maedel*," he said.

To which the baby smiled a second time. Oh, this was too much!

"*Ach*! Will you look at that?" *Dawdi* whispered.

Jonah gave a soft chuckle, the sound pleasant and surprising to Lovina. But inside, she felt deflated. For several days now, she'd been trying to get Autumn to smile, with absolutely no success. In walks Jonah, and the baby smiles twice for him.

He looked up at Lovina, his grin still firmly in place. "Did you see that, Lovina? Did you see? The *boppli* just smiled at me."

Lovina could only stare at him. His words and the way he said her name made her quiver inside. It was as if he wanted to share this important milestone with her. Like she mattered to him. Like she was his friend and companion. And how could she be angry with him when he acted like that?

She stood transfixed. Unable to move.

Barely able to breathe. She wanted to smile at him, too. Yes, it was wonderful that little Autumn had finally smiled for the first time. But Lovina was more fascinated with Jonah. Because he was smiling, too. She'd seen him do it before, at church and other gatherings when he'd been speaking to someone else. Usually from far across the room. Not up this close and personal. Not at her. But this time, his smile was for her alone. And for just a few moments, she felt as though they were the only two in the room. That no one existed in the whole wide world but them.

"Um, *ja*, I saw. That's amazing," she said, feeling awed by the event and completely unable to take her eyes off him.

Dawdi scooted closer, peering at the baby in anticipation. "See if you can get her to do it again."

Jonah turned and gave Autumn his full attention. "Can you smile for me again, sweet one?" he asked in his softest, most enticing tone.

A vision of the serpent beguiling Eve in the Garden of Eden flashed through Lovina's mind. Without intending to do so, she found herself smiling, too. And at that moment, she thought she might do anything for Jonah. Then she remembered who she was and who he was and that they weren't friends. Not really.

The baby rewarded Jonah for his effort, smiling so sweetly it brought tears to Lovina's eyes.

She turned away. The men's sudden laughter startled Autumn. Her eyes widened and her little chin quivered. Looking over her shoulder, Lovina wondered if the baby might cry.

"*Ach*, none of that, Itty-Bit. Everything is *allrecht*. There's no need for tears," Jonah soothed.

The baby settled right down, tracking Jonah's face as he reached for a burp cloth to wipe away a bit of drool from the corner of her mouth. Mesmerized, Lovina watched his movements.

"What a sweet *maedel*. It's too bad you can't keep her," *Dawdi* said.

Lovina's balloon popped. As if being propelled through a dark tunnel, she found herself back in reality. The future loomed before her like a great, hulking beast.

"*Ja*, it's too bad," Jonah said.

And Lovina realized she dreaded giving up the baby more than anything she'd faced yet.

"*Ach*, I better get this meal on. And you might as well join me for Thanksgiving dinner on Thursday, too. Unless you've been invited elsewhere?" She glanced at them, wondering what had possessed her to make the offer.

"*Ne*, we haven't been asked elsewhere. Most folks think you'll cook for us, so they don't invite us over for dinner anymore," *Dawdi* said.

Oh. No wonder old Marva Geingerich disapproved of Lovina living here on the farm. A single woman alone with two men. Even if they lived in separate houses and *Dawdi* was here to chaperone, it did seem a bit improper.

"I was planning to throw something together." *Dawdi* gave a little snicker but had the good grace to look a tad embarrassed. "We all know how that will work out. I'm not much of a cook but my Bertha could make anything. The best feasts I've ever eaten. We'd love to accept your invitation. It's awful kind of you to think of us, Lovina."

She merely nodded and stepped over to the stove. As she flipped off the burner and reached for the pot, she took a moment to wipe her eyes and gather her composure. Now she'd done it. Jonah would be here in her home on Thursday, but she'd rather eat with Jonah and his gentle grandfather than spend the holiday alone.

As she cut huge chunks of golden corn bread and placed them on the table, she couldn't help wondering what had just happened to her. A myriad of emotions coursed through her, and she couldn't make sense of it all.

She ladled stew into each of their bowls, realizing she'd shared something special with Jonah that most married people enjoyed with their own child. But they weren't married and never would be. Autumn was not their child. And against her better judgment, Lovina had invited these two men into her home to share Thanksgiving dinner with her. It was a time of peace, hope and gratitude. Yet she was filled with uncertainty. If she could have her Christmas wish, it would be for a *familye* of her own.

That thought brought a flood of warmth to her chest. How she longed to belong to someone. A *familye* who cared for her. Someone she could shower her love upon. But that wasn't possible. Not for her. Not ever again. She didn't deserve such exquisite joy. Especially not with a good, hardworking man like Jonah Lapp.

Oh, no! Not again! Jonah never should have let *Dawdi* drag him here to Lovina's kitchen for another meal. And now they were going to have Thanksgiving with her, too!

As he ate the hearty beef stew, his stomach rumbled with satisfaction. He couldn't deny she was one of the best cooks in the county. In fact, she seemed so good at everything she did. But he sensed something else was going on between them. Something he didn't understand. Because every time he was near Lovina Albrecht, he found himself feeling incredibly...

Confused!

An odd notion if ever he'd had one before. Lovina especially made him feel nervous. He had so many reservations about her. He told himself it wasn't because of her past. After all, *Dawdi* was right. Jonah didn't know all the details and wasn't in a position to judge her. Rather, he told himself that his misgivings were because of his own past. He didn't dare trust again. More than anything, he feared letting down his guard. He could never take that chance again.

"While I was working my EMT job this morning, I saw the bishop in town," Jonah said.

Lovina lifted her head and gazed at him.

"He said he'd received letters from three of the bishops in our region, and they know of no unwed *mudders* who might have run away. He hopes to hear from the other two bishops soon."

"What do you think is taking them so long to respond?" she asked.

Jonah shrugged. "I have no idea. Maybe they're making inquiries among their congregations."

Lovina frowned and he knew what she was thinking. The baby's mom obviously knew Lovina was a midwife. Only the Amish in their region would know who she was... unless word had traveled through the grapevine. The Amish were great letter writers and had lots of *familye* members they wrote to all the time. There were Mennonites but no Amish in New Mexico, Arizona or Utah that Jonah knew of. If Autumn's mom was from Kansas or Oklahoma, they might never find her, and Bishop Yoder would be forced to give the baby to another *familye*.

"We'll wait as long as it takes." Lovina ducked her head over her bowl.

They continued their meal in silence. Not unusual since they'd all worked hard and were hungry. Jonah held the baby easily with his left arm, listening to her little coos and gurgles as she waved her tiny arms. She smelled nice and he realized Lovina took excellent care of her. He worried what would happen to her when she left. Would her mom take as good care of her as Lovina did? Would her other *familye* protect her as they should? Would they love and teach her right? Oh, how he was going to miss her once Bishop Yoder took her away.

Likewise, he fretted over Lovina, too. He'd seen the newspaper and rental ads spread across her table when he'd come inside the house. From the big red circles drawn around several listings, he knew she was actively looking for another place to live. And where would that be? Maybe she could rent a room from another Amish *familye* in their *Gmay*. Without an examination room and nursery, that would make it difficult for her midwifery business. She might rent a house in town, which wasn't to his liking. She was a woman alone. Though she was independent and strong, she was also vulnerable. He didn't want someone to take advantage or hurt her. He wouldn't be there to protect her. And though it wasn't his business, he still worried about her. And that realization shook him to the core. Because caring led to an open heart that could be hurt.

"I… I better get out to the barn. I've got a few more chores I need to take care of." He scraped his chair back and stood, placing the baby in her bassinet.

Lovina looked up in surprise, holding her spoon aloft. "I've got pumpkin pies coming out of the oven in a few minutes, if you'd like a slice for dessert."

He shook his head. Though his mouth watered at the thought, he'd already consumed two huge bowls of tasty stew and chunks of buttered corn bread and his stomach was full. It was time to get back to work. He needed to put some distance between him and Lovina. Right now!

"What chores do you need to do? I thought we were through for the evening," *Dawdi* said, his forehead crinkled in a bewildered frown.

"I… I forgot to check the water troughs. Ice might have formed over the top, which will keep the horses and pigs from being able to drink."

Okay, it was a lame excuse but still very true.

"I checked them and everything's fine," *Dawdi* said.

Jonah's mind scattered. Both Grandpa and Lovina were sitting there, gazing at him with confused expressions.

"*Ach*, I also need to chop more firewood for the morning," he said.

There! That was good.

"Can't you do that in the morning?" *Dawdi* asked.

Yes, he could.

"It's nice to have it done and ready to go," he said.

Like him, Lovina was an early riser and he wanted to keep her supplied with kindling. After all, she had a new baby to tend. If nothing else, he was fastidious and took his work seriously. He rarely left things undone and liked to get a head start.

He stood at the back door, his hand on the knob as he threw a quick glance at Lovina. "*Danke* for supper."

"You're *willkomm*."

Her voice sounded quiet and subdued. Maybe she was uncomfortable with him here and wanted him to leave, too.

Conscious of the chilly breeze on the baby, he opened the door just a bit and stepped outside. He hurried and closed it tight again, then hustled over to the woodpile. It was dark outside but the round moon provided enough light for him to split several chunks. Even though he wasn't wearing his winter coat, he didn't feel the cold night air. He'd been well-warmed by Lovina's delicious stew and cheery kitchen. Although the farmhouse belonged to him, he'd started thinking of it as her place. Her home. She seemed to have settled right in, and it was obvious she didn't want to leave. And for the first time since she'd moved in, he found himself wishing she could stay. That they could keep Autumn for their own and be a real *familye*.

Ah, that would never work. They both had complicated pasts that haunted them. He didn't know Lovina's full story, but he was astute enough to see the pain in her eyes whenever she talked about her life. She'd been hurt deeply, just like him. But he didn't dare let down his guard with her. It was less painful to remain a bachelor. And yet the thought of Lovina moving away and never being able to see her bothered him greatly. Instead, he wished he could tell her that Autumn would stay with them forever. That everything was going to be all right. But it wasn't. And he didn't dare get involved. He couldn't make this right for any of them.

Chapter Ten

Lovina knocked forcefully on the front door of the *dawdi haus*. It was just past one o'clock in the morning and she should be fast asleep. Thick darkness gathered around her, the frigid air enfolding her quaking body. She was fully dressed but had forgotten her warm shawl. Yet she didn't feel the cold. Standing on Jonah's doorstep, all she could think about was little Autumn.

She pounded hard. "Jonah! Please, help!"

The door jerked open and she reared back in surprise. He stood before her wearing his pants and shirt. His feet were bare, his sand-colored hair askew. Obviously he'd dressed fast. He blinked his eyes, which were filled with sleep. She had no doubt she'd woken him.

"What is it?" he asked, his voice low and groggy.

"It's the *boppli*. Can you *komm* with me, please?" she asked.

She hated to disturb him. Hated to beg for help. If she wasn't in dire need, she never would have asked.

"What's wrong?" *Dawdi* called.

Lovina winced. Through the open doorway, she saw the older man standing in the threshold leading to his bedroom. It looked like she'd roused him, too. He was just pulling his black suspenders up over his shirt. His silvery hair was ruffled as he pushed his spectacles up on the bridge of his nose. Like Jonah, his feet were bare. Not so odd, considering it was the middle of the night.

Jonah raked a hand through his tousled hair and called over his shoulder. "Something's wrong with Autumn."

"Oh! You better go, then." A note of urgency filled *Dawdi*'s voice.

"*Ja, komm* quick. She's so sick," Lovina said, her voice sounding breathy and anxious to her own ears.

As she said the words, her heart skipped a beat, then pounded madly in her chest. The baby was ill and Lovina didn't know what to do. She couldn't lose another child.

"I'll be up at the farmhouse," Jonah called to his grandfather.

He reached for his boots sitting beside the front door and stomped his feet into them without socks. Grabbing his coat from the hook on the wall, he shrugged into it as he hurried into the night. Having completed her mission, Lovina literally sprinted back to the house. She hated leaving Autumn for even a moment and was eager to get back to the little girl. Jonah kept up with her all the way.

"What's the matter with her?" he asked when they stepped into her warm kitchen.

Lovina closed the door, then scurried to the back of the house where the nursery was located. "She's running a high temperature and has a deep, hacking cough. Over the past couple of days, I noticed she had a sniffly nose, but I didn't think it was serious. Now I'm worried."

Jonah was hot on her heels as they reached the baby's room. Lovina had turned on several gas-powered lamps. Autumn lay wheezing on her back in her rocking cradle. She was fussy, moving restlessly and flailing her tiny hands against her face, as if she didn't feel well. Now and then, she let out a miserable squall. And when she coughed, it sounded like a little dog barking.

"*Ach*, you poor *maedel*," Jonah said.

Lovina leaned over the child, resting a

hand against her tiny chest. She felt an edge of uncertainty. Thankfully, the baby's color looked good, and she seemed able to breathe well enough. But she kept coughing, a deep watery sound that Lovina knew was not good. As a midwife, she worked mainly with prenatal and postnatal issues. The babies she tended were usually newborns. She'd never had to deal with something like this and had no idea what was wrong.

"I don't know what to do," Lovina said.

"Here, let me."

Jonah crouched over the crib. He wasn't a doctor but as an EMT, he was called out on emergencies like this. While Lovina stood by, he quickly examined the baby from head to toe, then wrapped her up warm and lifted her to his shoulder.

"There, Itty-Bit. We're going to take *gut* care of you." His deep, soft voice seemed to calm the baby. And knowing he was here soothed Lovina's nerves, too.

"She's definitely hot to the touch. Have you taken her temperature in the last twenty minutes?" he asked.

Lovina nodded, filled with trepidation. "*Ja*, it's one hundred degrees on the dot."

"*Ach*, not too high yet."

Not too high? Considering Autumn was

two months old, Lovina thought it was in outer space.

Autumn coughed again, a heavy, crackling sound. What if she had pneumonia?

"What do you think is wrong with her? Is it just a bad cold?" Lovina asked. She twined her hands together, wishing she could do something.

"I think she has croup."

"Croup?" Lovina's voice squeaked with dismay.

"*Ja*, haven't you ever dealt with a croupy *boppli* before?"

"*Ne*, I help *mudders* with birthing issues. If their *boppli* is sick, I refer them immediately to a medical doctor at the hospital."

Also, Lovina had no children of her own. Though she had given birth once, she hadn't been able to raise her son.

"Where on earth would she have gotten croup from?" she asked.

Jonah shrugged. "Most likely from church. She is rather cute and everyone was oogling over her last Sunday. It's contagious among *kinder* and she could have easily picked it up then."

Oogling over her? If the situation wasn't so dire, Lovina would have laughed at his made-up word. Jonah was so serious all the time, except when it came to this baby. Then he was a giant teddy bear. And Lovina liked that about him, though she would never admit it out loud.

"Should we take her to a doctor?" Lovina asked.

Jonah frowned. "*Ne*, not yet. They'd ask questions about her parents, and we still don't want the *Englisch* involved. If all else fails, we could take her to Eli."

Eli Stoltzfus was an Amish paramedic in their *Gmay*. While an *Englisch* EMT drove the ambulance for them, Jonah frequently rode with Eli during their work shifts at the hospital. He was a nice man and Lovina trusted him. She had no doubt, if they were forced to take Eli into their confidence, he could be discreet and would help them protect Autumn and her mom from the *Englisch* authorities.

"I'd rather not involve more people in Autumn's situation without Bishop Yoder's permission. Let's see what we can do for the *boppli* on our own first," Jonah said.

Lovina didn't question him. They were Amish, after all. Self-sufficient and separate from the world. Even though they were certified as an EMT and midwife, they went to a doctor as a last resort. They also didn't want to lie when the *Englisch* medical staff asked them to fill out admitting paperwork. No doubt the form would include a place for the names of Autumn's parents, which meant they'd have to tell the truth and possibly lose the baby for good. But it was more serious than that. If the *Englisch* authorities discovered they'd had a baby abandoned into their care and hadn't turned her in, they could both lose their jobs. They might even face jail time. But worst of all, they would lose Autumn for good.

"What can I do?" Lovina asked.

"Have you got a warm hat for her?" he asked.

Filled with confusion, Lovina handed him a white yarn cap she'd knitted a week earlier. It was soft and warm for when she took Autumn with her to visit her expectant mothers.

"It's important we keep her as calm as possible." Jonah spoke as he tugged the cap onto Autumn's head. Then he bundled the baby up nice and warm with blankets, tucking her little hands and legs into the folds.

Carrying the *boppli* to the back door, Jonah spoke over his shoulder as Lovina followed. "Right now, I think we need some cool air to ease the swelling in her air passages."

"What? You mean, you're taking her outside? But it's freezing cold out there," Lovina said.

She couldn't believe he wanted to take Autumn outside. It was late and officially Thanksgiving Day. Christmas was right around the corner. Lovina didn't believe the cold night air was good for anyone, much less a young baby. She took Autumn's care quite seriously. If something happened to her, how could Lovina live with herself or explain it to Bishop Yoder?

"She's dressed warmly. The cool air will help diminish the inflammation in her air passages. We'll only go outside for a few minutes," Jonah said.

Determined not to let Autumn out of her sight, Lovina reached for a woolen shawl and dragged it over her shoulders as she stepped out onto the back porch with Jonah. The heavens above were black as coal, not a single star or moon to offer them light. They might have rain or another snowstorm by morning.

Jonah stood and rocked Autumn back and forth, comforting her. As he leaned his head over her, Autumn stared up at him with her wide eyes. So sick and vulnerable, yet so trusting. Now and then, she released a tight, low-pitched cough.

"We don't want her to get overly excited. That will only trigger more coughing spasms," Jonah explained, speaking quietly to Lovina.

Ah. Now she understood his whispers and slow, methodical movements. Jonah was so calm, so confident. He always seemed to know just what to do.

They stood there in the dark, their puffs of breath looking like gray smoke on the air. A dim light glimmered in the *dawdi haus* window, and Lovina knew *Dawdi* must have lit a kerosene lamp. She was sorry to wake everyone, but it couldn't be helped. After a few minutes, the baby closed her eyes and a blaze of panic gripped Lovina.

"Is she okay?" She reached out and touched the baby, searching for life.

Autumn jerked and began to fuss again but Jonah shushed her gently. "There, Itty-Bit. It's *allrecht*. You're going to be just fine. *Mammi* Lovina is just overly worried about you," Jonah said.

Yes. Lovina felt like a very worried mommy.

The baby settled again, and Jonah offered Lovina a reassuring smile. "You see? She's fine. She was just falling asleep. Notice she's stopped coughing? The cool air has helped quite a lot."

Lovina stared at him, her pulse racing, her

legs feeling weak as noodles. How could he remain so relaxed when she was frantic with fear?

"We can't stay out here in the cold much longer," she said.

"We won't. We'll take her to the bathroom and run hot water to get some nice moist air for her to breathe. It will help relax her vocal cords," he said.

"But what if it doesn't work? What if…?"

She couldn't finish. Absolute terror gripped her heart. She wasn't Autumn's mother but she felt like she was. For the past weeks, she'd been tending to the baby as though she were her own. And like any worried mom, Lovina feared the worst. She loved this baby. Heaven help her, she did! She knew Jonah did, too. And for one insane moment, she thought it was a shame they weren't Autumn's parents. That they weren't a *familye* for real.

"Lovina, stop worrying. She's going to be *allrecht*," he said again.

The way he said her name made her feel special for some odd reason. Like she could do anything as long as he was by her side.

He nodded at the door. "Let's take Autumn inside and run some hot water."

Lovina opened the screen for him, then stood back as he carried the baby inside. She scurried ahead to the bathroom and turned on the hot water. It took a moment for the water to warm up. She didn't have a humidifier, so this would have to do.

Sitting on a stool, Jonah pulled the shower curtain so it would hold the mist around the baby. With his strong arms, he held the girl close to the faucet as she breathed in the moist air.

"Let's keep the door closed as much as possible, to hold the steam in," he said.

Lovina nodded and closed the door before sitting on the edge of the bathtub. Soon, the condensation built up and water droplets ran down the sides of the walls and clung to every surface. She gazed at Jonah, drinking in his confidence. Letting his cool demeanor calm her frayed nerves. Then she studied the baby's face, ensuring herself that Autumn was still breathing. That she wasn't turning blue from lack of oxygen. Though Lovina had always taken pride in her calm, deliberate movements as a midwife, she now felt frenzied and out of control. She tried to quiet herself. To have faith and trust in the Lord. And as they sat there, she prayed, asking *Gott* to bless Autumn and help them know how to care for the little girl.

Over the next few hours, they took turns

holding the baby over the tub. Though the girl was small, Lovina's arms gave out after some time. Jonah seemed to know exactly when to take Autumn from her. With his strong arms, he held the child easily, showing no fatigue. His kind patience impressed Lovina. She realized with a bit of dismay that if Jonah wasn't here, she wouldn't have a clue what to do. She'd be lost without him. And that's when she knew she loved him, though she didn't know how it had happened. She loved him and he was leaving and her heart would be broken once more.

Before sunrise, she took the baby's temperature again. It was still high.

"I'm afraid this isn't enough," Lovina said.

"If her fever hasn't broken and she's not breathing easier by daybreak, I'll get the buggy ready and we'll take her to Eli or the hospital. A doctor would probably give her a steroid to help her fight the illness," he said.

"Can't you give her the steroid?"

Jonah shook his head. "I don't have any here at the farm. Eli might have some but his farm is seven miles away. It'd be quicker to take Autumn to the hospital in town. Either way, she's a very young *boppli*. I'd rather not administer medications unless we must."

Lovina nodded. They'd done everything

they could for the child. Now it was up to *Gott*. But the stakes were high. To save the baby's life, they would visit Eli or an *Englisch* doctor…and possibly lose their jobs in the process.

"How long will this croup last?" Lovina asked.

She was holding Autumn at this point and cradled the child close against her chest while keeping the baby's face turned toward the warm, moist air. In a moment of dismay, she realized the steam had wilted her hair and clothes, and she had damp tendrils sticking to her face. With her hands occupied, she couldn't even push them back. Jonah must think she looked a sight.

Jonah shrugged. "Two or three days. But I think we're making progress already."

"*Ja*, she's not coughing as much."

And what a relief. Obviously Jonah knew what he was doing, but Lovina didn't believe they were out of the woods yet.

Throughout the night, they kept their vigil over the baby. At one point, Lovina passed the child back to Jonah and went out to the kitchen to make them a cup of hot chocolate. She offered Autumn a bottle, but the baby wouldn't take it.

Hours later, the hot water tank was drained

and Autumn's fever finally broke. She was breathing easy and sleeping peacefully.

Lovina carried the baby into the living room, satisfied the danger had passed. Jonah was slumped awkwardly in a nearby chair that was way too small for his long frame. His handsome face softened in sleep, his full lips parted as he breathed in repose. Like her, he must be exhausted.

Dawdi Noah lay sprawled across the sofa, his soft snores filling the air. Lovina had no idea when the elderly man had come inside the house. Jonah must have let him in and explained what was going on. Though both men were asleep, it brought Lovina a great deal of comfort having them near. Against her better judgment, she'd grown fond of them both.

A faint spray of sunlight gleamed through the wide picture windows. Lovina had made plain brown curtains and hung them there just a month earlier. When she'd moved into this house, she'd known it wasn't forever but she had adopted it as her semipermanent home. Now she wondered where she would go. Previous to living here, she'd rented a room from the Schwartz *familye*. But Hannah was expecting again and they needed the space for their own kids. The Burkholders' eldest daughter had just married and moved to Westcliffe. Maybe they had room for her. But Lovina dreaded another temporary home. She wanted a place of her own.

A glint of sunbeams landed squarely on Jonah's angular profile. A lock of hair hung over his forehead and she was tempted to reach out and push it back. She resisted the urge, knowing the movement would awaken him.

For several minutes, she gazed at his relaxed face, unable to understand the warm feelings cascading through her heart. And though it made her feel all mushy inside, she forced herself to think about the baby instead. She couldn't let down her guard. She'd fought too hard for her independence to lose it now. Jonah was selling his farm. Soon Lovina would find a new place to live. And once Jonah moved back east, they'd never see each other again. And yet she couldn't help wishing for more.

By late afternoon, Jonah sat in Lovina's kitchen, watching her mash potatoes in a tall cooking pot. The air smelled of roast turkey, stuffing and fresh yeast rolls. In spite of being up all night with a sick baby, she'd managed to cook them a Thanksgiving feast.

Holding Autumn in his arms, Jonah saw she was asleep. He was tempted to put her in her cradle and help Lovina, yet he was loath to do so. He wanted to keep the child close until he was positive she was safe. The baby's fever had finally broken and her cough diminished quite a bit, yet he was worried. What if it flared up again? What if she had pneumonia?

A loud clatter in the sink caused him to snap his head up. The baby jerked and her eyes fluttered open, then closed again. She didn't even cry, indicating how badly she needed rest.

"I'm sorry," Lovina said.

She looked over her shoulder at him, her hands gripping the potato pot. The slump of her shoulders and black circles beneath her eyes attested to her exhaustion. Last night, she'd done everything he asked without hesitation. And her trust touched his heart like nothing else could. For just a moment he imagined Fannie in the same situation and doubted she would have handled the baby's illness as well as Lovina.

Standing, he stepped into the living room and laid the baby in her cradle. He'd moved the tiny bed there last night. She'd be close enough that they could hear her breathing and check on her often, yet not so close that the noises in the kitchen would disturb her.

Lovina struggled to lift the heavy turkey out of the oven. With three of them for dinner, he wondered why she'd baked such a large bird. His mouth watered in anticipation of the yummy leftovers. Then he reconsidered. Until he sold the farm, this was Lovina's home. Her kitchen. Her turkey. He doubted he'd get to enjoy the remnants later tonight or tomorrow.

"Let me." Brushing her hands aside, he took the oven mitts and lifted the bird over to the counter for her.

"Danke," she said.

He inclined his head. Working side by side, they drained the drippings into another pan. While Lovina stirred together a tasty gravy, Jonah sliced the juicy meat.

The back screen door creaked and Jonah looked up. *Dawdi* came inside, carrying a bucket of firewood.

"Ach! It's a cold one. I had to chop ice off the watering trough so the cows could drink." The old man limped over to the far wall and set the bucket down. There was no resentment in his cheery voice.

"I'm sorry, *Dawdi*. I should be out there working. You should be inside where it's warm," Jonah said.

He reached for his jacket. He'd been so

wound up helping Lovina and the baby that he'd almost forgotten his responsibilities on the farm.

Dawdi waved a gnarled hand in the air. "Don't worry yourself. There's nothing left to do today. I got all the livestock fed and the cows milked. I even gathered the eggs and put them in the fridge. We can clean them later, after we've had our Thanksgiving dinner."

Jonah glanced around the kitchen. Lovina had spread a plain white tablecloth and set out the dishes. In the center of the table, she'd laid small orange pumpkins and white and yellow gourds. Simple, yet colorful for the season. It added a festive look to the table and pleased him for some odd reason.

"How's the *boppli*?" *Dawdi* asked, keeping his normally loud voice low as he peered into the living room.

"She's doing *gut*, thanks to Jonah," Lovina said.

Setting a large drumstick on the meat platter, Jonah blinked in surprise. He appreciated Lovina's trust, yet it was a confidence he didn't feel. Last night, he'd kept it together for her and the baby's sake. After all, he was an EMT and it would do none of them good to panic. But inside, he'd never been so afraid. What if Autumn had died while in their care?

How could he ever live with himself if he lost that little girl? How could he explain himself to Bishop Yoder?

Setting the meat on the table, he hurried into the other room to check Autumn. She was sleeping and breathing easy. Nothing to be alarmed about.

When he turned, he bumped into Lovina. She leaned over his shoulder, her eyebrows pulled together in concern. She stood so close that he caught the subtle fragrance of her coconut shampoo. Their eyes met and her soft breath brushed against his chin. For several pounding moments, he felt suspended in time.

"Is she *allrecht*?" Lovina whispered.

"*Ja*. She's fine. I just wanted to make sure before we start our meal," he said.

A movement caught his eye, and he turned toward the doorway. *Dawdi* stood there smiling softly, his eyes filled with knowing curiosity.

Lovina nodded and turned back to the kitchen, wiping her hands on the apron around her waist. Jonah followed, feeling warm and flushed.

"I think we're ready to eat," Lovina said.

She set a bowl of steaming gravy beside the potatoes and corn along with two kinds of homemade preserves and a colorful fruit salad. They each took their seats and waited for *Dawdi*, who was the eldest and would fill the role of head of the household.

"*Danke* for this great feast, Lovina. It looks *wundervoll*. Let us pray and give thanks," *Dawdi* said.

Lovina smiled graciously and they all bowed their heads. After a few moments, they ate quietly. Jonah figured they were too tired for much conversation. He couldn't help feeling grateful. They'd had a frightening night but Autumn was doing well. They had plenty of food on the table and a warm home to live in. Surely the Lord had blessed them. So why did Jonah feel anxious and nervous? Why couldn't he find peace in his heart?

Why did he want to leave?

The question made him pause. Since Fannie had broken their engagement, he'd longed to escape. To live anywhere but here. But now he wasn't sure.

The baby coughed and they turned toward the doorway, their eating utensils suspended in midair. Lovina immediately popped out of her chair but Jonah held out a hand to stop her. She hovered there, looking anxious.

"Her cough sounds looser. I think she's over the worst of it," Jonah said.

Autumn quieted and Lovina sat down

again, releasing a little sigh. Like him, she was worried and unwilling to leave anything to chance. Yet he knew that right now the baby needed sleep more than anything.

They resumed their meal, rounding it off with thick wedges of pumpkin pie and sweet cream. After so much preparation, now came the cleanup.

Sitting in the rocking chair in the living room, *Dawdi* fed a little milk to Autumn while Jonah helped Lovina wash the dishes.

"*Danke* for all your assistance last night and today," she said as she rinsed another plate and set it in the drain.

Wielding a clean dish towel, Jonah dried a glass and set it aside. "It's no problem. I'm just happy it's all worked out. I was just doing what the bishop asked."

She glanced at him, a slight frown on her face. For a fraction of a moment, he saw some emotion in her beautiful blue eyes. Doubt or regret, he wasn't sure which. Maybe a little of both. Then she looked away, and he thought he must have imagined it. But he couldn't help feeling as if he'd said something wrong. Something that bothered Lovina. A lot.

He gazed at her soft profile. A lock of golden hair had come loose from her prayer *kapp* and lay against her soft cheek. The curl trembled slightly with every exhale she took. He was tempted to reach out and touch that silky texture. To gently tuck it back behind her ear. But he didn't dare. Because it was much too personal and might give her the wrong idea. After all, he was selling the farm and would be leaving the area soon.

For several minutes, Jonah gazed at Lovina's sweet face. He forced himself not to give in and tell her what he was thinking. Over the past few months since she'd moved into his farmhouse, they'd worked together. Caring for Lovina's expectant mothers and little Autumn. He couldn't deny they'd grown close. But that was just one more reason for him to distance himself from her as fast as possible. He could never tell her his thoughts. Never confide in her. That would only make him vulnerable to being hurt again.

Once the kitchen was tidy, he stepped toward the back door, eager to flee.

"I better check on the livestock. If you or Autumn need anything else, anything at all, just call," he said.

Lovina blinked, seeming surprised by his sudden departure. Today was a day for eating too much, giving thanks and visiting. Not a day for work. But Jonah felt if he didn't get out of here right now, he might explode.

"*Ach*, I know we're all tired. *Danke* again. You've been such a great help," she said.

Looking away, he hardened his heart and purposefully pushed aside his riotous feelings of frustration and regret. He wanted to smile and talk and stay right here with her, but that would only prove fatal to his peace of mind. Instead, he focused on his goals. He was going to sell this farm and move back east where he could forget his broken heart once and for all.

Chapter Eleven

Ten days later, Autumn had recovered from her croup and was doing well. It was the second week of December and two inches of snow blanketed the ground. Long icicles clung to the edges of the farmhouse gutters. The early-morning air was brisk, a chilly breeze blowing from the north. The sun blazed brilliantly in the sky. Little Autumn was down for her morning nap, and Lovina had taken advantage of the good weather. Standing in the backyard, she had just finished hanging her clean laundry on the line, knowing the icicles would melt and her clothes would be freeze-dried by late afternoon. That would give her enough clean diapers for Autumn to last several days.

As she finished the chore, a horse and buggy came down the lane. After dropping the unused clothespins into a plastic bucket, she picked up her laundry basket and skirted the house. As usual, Jonah had shoveled the paths and they were almost dry.

Bracing the basket against her right hip, she stood there and waited. David Troyer, one of her expectant fathers, pulled his buggy to a halt beside the house and jumped out in an energetic bound. His black felt hat was askew and he wore a warm winter coat, scarf, black leather gloves and boots.

Lovina's senses perked into overdrive. "David! What are you doing here? Is everything *allrecht*?"

"*Ach*, Lovina! I'm so glad you're here. It's Millie's time. You've got to *komm* with me," he said.

Lovina forced herself to remain calm. This was Millie's first baby and she wasn't due for three weeks. It could be a false alarm.

"How often are her contractions?" Lovina asked.

"Every three to five minutes. I timed them, just like you showed me," he said.

"And how long are they lasting?"

"About sixty seconds."

Yes, it was time to go. Carrying the basket, Lovina walked briskly toward the house. Whether Millie was really in labor or not,

Lovina would hurry to her side. She spoke over her shoulder as she hurried along. "I'll get my medical bag and be right with you. Jonah should be working out in the barn. Can you get him for me, please?"

Since she had to travel to the Troyers' farm by buggy, she shouldn't delay. During her husband's absence, Millie's contractions would have increased. Millie's mother was staying with her, so she wasn't alone, but the baby might be coming early. Lovina needed to get there and ensure everything was all right.

But what should she do with Autumn? If Millie's baby really was coming, Lovina wanted Jonah to accompany her, just in case there were complications. He could tend to Millie while Lovina cared for the premature baby.

Autumn was doing great since her illness but Lovina hated to take her out into the cold air quite yet. Maybe *Dawdi* would be willing to keep an eye on her.

Inside the farmhouse, Lovina set the laundry basket on the kitchen table. Opening the fridge, she scanned the baby bottles she'd prepared earlier that morning and did a quick assessment. There was plenty of milk for Autumn to last through the day and night. Hopefully, she'd be back by morning to prepare some more. If not, *Dawdi* would be on his own to milk the goats and process the milk for the baby. It wouldn't be ideal but Lovina knew he could do it. She'd learned that *Dawdi* and Jonah did what had to be done without grumbling about it.

In the living room, she gathered up her medical bag, which she always kept packed and ready to go at a moment's notice. As she turned toward the kitchen, Jonah knocked, then entered the back door already dressed in his warm winter clothes. *Dawdi* Noah and David accompanied him.

"David says Millie's gone into labor and you wanted to see me," Jonah said.

Lovina set her bag on the table. "*Ja*, she's three weeks early. Can you accompany me? I want to ensure we provide the best care possible, in case there are difficulties."

"Of course. I've already harnessed the horse and buggy and can leave the moment you're ready." Jonah dipped his head in acknowledgment.

"I can look after Autumn while you're gone," *Dawdi* offered.

Lovina stepped over to the older man and gripped his hand with affection as she gazed into his eyes. "I was hoping you'd offer. I don't want to take the *boppli* out so soon after her illness. There are plenty of bottles of milk already prepared in the fridge. She ate about an hour ago. I don't know how long I'll be. It could be a long birth. And if there are complications, I'll need to stay with Millie."

Dawdi straightened his sagging shoulders and nodded, no hesitation in his eyes. "I understand. I can do it. I know how to warm up a bottle for Autumn. I raised my own *kinder* and I've watched you do it often enough."

She smiled, her heart filled with love for this kind old man. "I have no doubt you know what to do. But if Millie's labor is long and keeps me away until tomorrow, you might have to milk the goats."

"Don't worry! It's no problem." The man looked perfectly serious and ready to accept this assignment.

It occurred to Lovina at that moment that *Dawdi* liked being included. And she didn't ask why. No matter how old a person got, they still liked to feel loved, wanted and needed.

"The *boppli* is down for a nap and should sleep another hour. I've got more diapers drying on the clothesline and some leftovers from a nice chicken-and-dumpling casserole in my fridge. Help yourself," she said.

Dawdi smiled wide at that. "*Ach*, that's kind of you."

No doubt he was pleased with the prospect of not having to cook today.

"You're *willkomm*, *Dawdi*. I really need your help right now, and I so appreciate your willingness to do this for me," she said.

"It's my pleasure."

"Let's go then!" An anxious-looking David opened the back door.

Jonah picked up Lovina's medical bag. She stepped outside and he took her elbow, as if he feared she might slip and fall. And though she was surprised by the gesture, she didn't shrug him off as he accompanied her to their buggy. David climbed into his own buggy and they followed him.

The journey took forty minutes. While Jonah put the horses in the barn, Lovina hurried into the house with David. Since she'd been here many times before, she went straight to the back bedroom. Millie sat up in the narrow bed, a plethora of pillows supporting her back. Her mother, Iris Miller, stood beside the bed, wringing out a wet cloth.

"Lovina! I'm so glad you're here," Millie cried, her face damp with sweat.

Lovina went right over to the young mother and squeezed her hand, giving her a warm smile of encouragement as she checked her pulse. "*Ja*, I'm here. How are you doing?"

"I'm okay but it's too early. I told David I couldn't be in labor yet. It's just those early contractions you warned me about. Isn't it?" Her voice sounded rather breathless.

Opening her medical bag, Lovina took out her blood pressure cuff, fetal Doppler and stethoscope. "Let's find out."

After checking Millie's blood pressure, she waited for the young mother to have another contraction, then checked the fetal heart tones. A quick exam confirmed that the baby was in the right position to be born.

"*Ja*, you are definitely in labor. You are going to have a sweet little *boppli* in the coming hours," Lovina said.

Iris reached to hold her daughter's hand. "What can I do to help?"

Lovina patted the older woman's shoulder. "If you can continue to swab Millie's face and neck, I think that will provide her a great deal of comfort right now."

David stepped to the other side of the bed. A sweet feeling washed over Lovina as she watched him lean over and kiss his wife's forehead and whisper gentle words of encouragement to her.

At that moment, Jonah stepped into the room, carrying his own medical bag.

"Is there anything I can do?" he asked quietly.

His gaze rested on the loving couple but he hung back, as if he didn't want to intrude. After all, Millie was giving birth and he was somewhat of an outsider.

"Could you heat some hot water for me?" Lovina asked.

Iris frowned. "I'll do that."

Tossing Jonah a disapproving glance, the older woman bustled past him and hurried into the kitchen. Obviously she didn't like him being here. Even though she knew he was an EMT, for some Amish, childbirth was a woman's art and not to involve a man.

Taking the hint, Jonah shrank back, speaking in a quiet tone. "I don't want to interfere. I'll wait out here. If you need anything at all, just holler."

Lovina nodded. This was her area of expertise, yet she still liked having him around. Especially if something went wrong.

She went to work laying out her instruments and preparing the room just as she liked it for a birth setting. Iris returned minutes later and Lovina kept her busy. Though he stayed out of the way, Jonah anticipated

Lovina's every need. While she laid out extra under-pads and clean sheets, she asked him to set up the oxygen and accessories, then hang a plastic trash bag on the door handle. Though he wasn't a father, he knew what to do and she was impressed by his knowledge and sensitivity to the process.

David focused on his wife, seeing to her comfort, offering support through each contraction. And in between, he offered Millie a few crackers to eat and sips of water as Lovina directed. Millie panted through each painful spasm, the couple working together like a team. The tender way David massaged his wife's shoulders and back reminded Lovina there were still good men in the world.

Kind men like Jonah.

She assessed the baby's heartbeat every half hour. Everything proceeded like clockwork…until Millie felt like pushing. Then she gasped and spewed through the first agonizing contraction and the next. At this rate, Lovina realized Millie would become too exhausted to last.

"Let your body do the work and try to breathe gently through your nose. Don't let air escape your lips. Put that energy into pushing. That will make the process easier on your *boppli*," she encouraged.

Millie nodded obediently, then her face was torn by another painful grimace. As instructed, she kept her mouth closed, her face contorting with focused pain. Over the next few hours, the young mother labored to bring her child into the world. And though everything appeared to be proceeding as it should, Lovina became concerned. Millie's labor was not progressing. There was no movement. And that could take too great a toll on both Millie and her baby.

"I had all my *bopplin* fast," Iris kept saying. "I popped them right out."

Lovina let the woman talk, using it as a distraction for poor Millie. But she stepped over to the doorway and quietly gestured to Jonah.

He glanced into the room. He ducked his head as he listened to her quiet whispers.

"Millie's heart rate is strong but I'm concerned about the *boppli*. I'm seeing signs of distress in the fetal heart rate," she explained.

He nodded. "What would you like me to do?"

Because she'd already done her homework, Lovina knew the nearest telephone was only one mile down the road at the Watson farm. The Watsons were *Englisch* but they were good neighbors and knew Millie was expecting. If Jonah showed up on their doorstep, they had already said they would gladly let him use their phone to call an ambulance.

Darkness filled the top of the windowsill, telling Lovina it was late at night. No doubt the road was dark and slick by now. She hated to send him out before morning but they both would do what was necessary for the safety of Millie and her baby.

"I'm going to give it another twenty minutes, and if Millie's labor hasn't progressed by that time, I'll ask you to go to the Watsons' farm and call an ambulance," she said.

She didn't feel the need to explain. With his training, Jonah knew exactly what to expect and how to proceed. After all, they'd been in situations like this before and she knew she could depend on him.

He nodded. "I'll be ready the moment you give me the word."

She took a deep inhale and offered a silent prayer. But as she swiveled around to return to Millie's side, Jonah did something completely unexpected. He squeezed her hand.

"It'll be *allrecht*," he said.

She looked at him, feeding off his kind words. How did he always know exactly what she needed to hear? It was as if he knew her thoughts and feelings.

"Danke," she said.

As she worked with Millie to coax her baby into the light, Lovina took comfort in knowing *Gott* had a plan for each of them. She felt Him in that room, guiding her every move. Another fifteen minutes passed. Finally, in a mad rush, the baby slid into David's capable hands.

"It's a *maedel*," he crowed with delight, a grin as big as Kansas plastered across his face.

Both Millie and Iris laughed out loud. Then Millie wept tears of absolute joy.

"Ach, she's so beautiful," Lovina said.

She instructed David to deliver the squalling newborn to her mother's chest. Millie clutched her baby close and kissed the top of her daughter's head.

"She's lovely," she said.

"She has a *gut* pair of lungs, that's for sure," Lovina said.

Her pronouncement was meant to put the new parents at ease but was also an assessment of the baby's health. Since the little girl was born early, Lovina was watching for any signs of distress.

"There, there," Millie cooed, trying to calm her child.

Iris stood close by, admiring the little girl's fine features. "She looks just like Millie when she was born. Not a bit of hair on her head."

They all laughed, and Lovina took several minutes to appreciate the miracle of life. While she unobtrusively tended to Millie's needs, she let the *familye* talk and bask in the joy of new parenthood. And soon, the child calmed as she quietly nursed.

"Since it's Christmastime, we'll name her Mary in honor of the Christ child's *mudder*," David said.

Millie looked up at her husband with complete devotion and smiled with pleasure. "Mary. *Ach*, that's a fine name."

Lovina thought so, too. Looking up, she saw Jonah standing in the doorway, a soft smile curving his fine mouth. Their gazes met and held for several profound moments. And just then, Lovina basked in the soft glow of love filling the air. She also felt a sudden and deep sorrow in her heart.

She looked away. This was her work. It was Jonah's work, too. They were both trained to deal with situations like this. Lovina was glad to share the joy of a successful delivery with him, and yet a dark cloud hung over them. Because she was soon moving out of his farmhouse. They wouldn't be working together anymore. Especially when he sold his farm and moved far, far away. And that thought left her bereft.

"I hope Dawdi is doing okay with Autumn. Do you think the two of them are *allrecht*?"

Jonah jerked his head to the side and glanced at Lovina. She sat beside him in the buggy. They were headed home after a successful birth at the Troyers'. The soft glow of sunrise filtered over the Wet Mountains and glimmered off the surrounding snow-covered fields in a cascade of sparkling diamonds. Though they'd been up all night, he wasn't tired at all. Instead, he felt light and victorious. Like he could conquer anything in the world.

"*Ja*, I'm sure they're both fine," he said.

Spindly tree limbs, devoid of any leaves, outlined the county road. The cold December morning was crisp but clear. To fight off the chill, they'd bundled up beneath two warm quilts. Hunkered securely within the confines of the buggy, Jonah could see the frost of their exhales, yet it felt quite warm. The cheery sound of sleigh bells filled the air with each step of the trotting horse. *Dawdi* had put the bells on the harness several days earlier. The bells reminded Jonah that Christmas was just a few weeks away. This season marked the Savior's birth. A time of hope and joy. But Jonah had never cared for the holidays much. And yet he'd just shared an amazing experience with Lovina. The miracle of birth. Something he'd participated in a number of times before. But this time, it seemed more personal and real.

"You're awfully quiet this morning. What are you thinking about?" she asked.

"I… I was just pondering little Mary's birth and how appropriate it was for this time of year. It was a nice reminder as we prepare to celebrate the birth of Jesus Christ," he said.

Okay, maybe he shouldn't have said that, but he was feeling a bit sentimental today.

"You're so right. I'm glad everything worked out *allrecht*," Lovina said. "Little Mary is eating and breathing well on her own and seems perfectly healthy. Even though she was born three weeks early, she weighs a *gut* six pounds and two ounces."

"*Ja*, that's a sound enough weight for a newborn," he agreed with a laugh.

"I weighed just under five pounds when I was born," she said.

He quirked his eyebrows up. "Really? That's quite tiny."

"Uh-huh. My *mamm* said I came two weeks early. How much did you weigh?" she asked.

He shrugged, the question taking him off guard. "I have no idea. My *mudder* wasn't around to ask."

Lovina was quiet for a moment. "I'm sorry, Jonah."

"Don't be. It's not your fault. I just wish she'd stuck around. There's so much I want to ask her. So many things I'd like to learn. As it is, I still don't know what she was like or anything about her. I have no idea why she left. I don't even know who my father was."

"*Dawdi* doesn't know either?" she asked.

He gripped the lead lines tighter. "*Ne*. My *mudder* told him my *vadder* was *Englisch* and didn't want us. That's all she would say. But none of us know where she went. It haunts me, you know? Wondering about her. And more than anything, I hate the thought that Autumn might suffer the same fate."

Okay, he'd just confided too much. And yet Lovina was so easy to talk to. Right now, he felt as though he could tell her anything. But he mustn't. He'd been hurt enough and didn't want to open up his heart again.

"I'm sorry for your heartache," she said.

"But you're a *gut* man, Jonah Lapp. You serve the Lord willingly. Your *dawdi* and *mammi* loved and raised you. You're a hard worker and have a nice farm. You're a member of our Amish faith and have so much to be grateful for. Your *dawdi* is so proud of you."

She was right, of course. Yet he still felt deficient somehow. There was an emptiness inside him that couldn't be filled.

"My farm is too small," he said.

She shrugged. "Maybe so, but it is beautiful."

"You really think so?" he asked.

"*Ja*, I do. I've never been happier than while I've been living there."

Her words stunned him to the core. "But I can't grow enough feed for my own livestock. I have to work at the hospital to make ends meet," he said.

The confession was difficult for him. He'd never forget how disappointed Fannie had been when he'd told her. Though they'd been engaged to marry at the time, she'd gotten real quiet and wouldn't look at him. When he'd taken her home, she'd avoided his kiss good-night. Three days later, she'd broken off their engagement. She'd married Alvin a month after that. Alvin, whose *familye* owned the largest farm in the area, with plenty of money to go around.

"But you're making ends meet, right?" Lovina asked. "You've overcome the obstacles and made your place a great success. Besides, you're so talented that you have other options to earn a living. That's why you're an EMT. And you provide a great service to our community. Your farm is where you live but you're able to bring money in from other places, too. And anyway, you don't want to put all your eggs in one basket. It's best to have income from several different sources."

He stared at her, stunned to the tips of his toes. Her optimism was insightful. He'd never looked at it like that, but she was right. Instead of seeing the bad, he should focus on the good.

"And don't worry about Autumn," she continued. "We're going to ensure she grows up feeling loved and wanted. She's not alone. She'll always have us," she said.

Us. The word seemed so final. So united. But once the bishop took the baby and gave her to another *familye*, she wouldn't have them anymore.

"I wanted to keep my *boppli*," Lovina said, her voice a broken whisper filled with longing. "My boyfriend was barely fifteen years old…way too young to support us. But after the birth, I was determined to keep my *sohn* anyway."

"Why didn't you?" Jonah asked.

She didn't look at him. "I was too young and it was a difficult birth. I was exhausted. If only I hadn't fallen asleep. My *vadder* took my child away in the middle of the night. And when I awoke and discovered what he'd done, I was beside myself. I tried to find my *sohn* without success. But to this day, I still mourn his loss. I have no idea if he's growing up feeling loved and wanted or sad and neglected. I can only have faith that *Gott* is watching over him. I have to put my trust in the Lord. And that's what you should do, too."

Jonah stared straight ahead. He was surprised and torn by her words. They were the last thing he'd expected to hear.

"I didn't realize you wanted to keep your *boppli*," he said.

"Of course I did! I would have raised him," she cried. "He'd still be with me now. If only my *vadder* hadn't taken him away. But my *daed* was so angry. I was young and stupid, Jonah. Too young to realize the pain and trouble I caused with my actions. My *daed* said I'd brought shame to our entire *familye*. He took my little *bu* away and refused to tell me where he'd gone. Then my *vadder* left us, too."

Lovina's words made Jonah feel rotten inside. She'd been abandoned just like him. His heart gave a painful squeeze when he thought of the grief she must have suffered. The loss and humiliation she must have felt. Jonah's grandparents had never made him feel ashamed or unwanted. He could only imagine what Lovina had gone through at the hands of her disapproving father.

"Like a hypocrite, my *vadder* left our faith and joined the *Englisch* world and married some *Englisch* woman," Lovina said. "And the worst part about it was that my *mudder* could never remarry. You know the tenets of our faith. Even with a divorce, it's considered adultery to marry as long as your ex-spouse is still alive. I watched my poor *mudder* work herself into an early grave so she could provide for me."

He glanced at her. "Surely our *Gmay* helped her?"

"*Ja*, as much as they could. But she refused charity. I think she died of a broken heart."

Lovina buried her face in her hands, her shoulders trembling with silent tears. Jonah hesitated. Then he reached out and rested a hand on her arm, trying to comfort her.

"You've suffered so much, Lovina. More than I ever knew. And I... I've judged you unfairly. I'm so very sorry," he said.

She sniffled and lifted her head. Her nose and eyes were red. "It's okay. I've learned to live with it. I've moved on and tried to make the best of what *Gott* has given me. I don't usually cry about it but I'm overly tired today, so my guard is down."

"Have you really gotten over it? Losing your little *bu*, I mean?" he asked.

She glanced his way and he saw the trickle of tears as they ran down her cheeks. She shook her head. "*Ne*, I don't think I'll ever get over losing my *boppli*."

Ah, how he hated to see her cry. She'd been victimized by her father. It wasn't her fault. She'd wanted to do what she thought was right. To make things good and raise her baby on her own. But her dad wouldn't let her. And knowing this filled Jonah with the desire to protect Lovina and always keep her safe. He knew he could change the future for them both. The two of them didn't have to be sad and lonely anymore. They didn't have to let the bishop take Autumn away. Not when he could do something about it.

"We need to talk," Jonah said.

In a spontaneous act, he pulled the horse

and buggy over to the side of the road. The sun was burning the frost off the asphalt. No doubt *Dawdi* was weary after caring for Autumn all night long. Jonah needed to get home and take care of his farm chores so *Dawdi* wouldn't feel obligated to do them. But first…

"What are you doing?" Lovina asked as she wiped her eyes.

He faced her, reaching to gently clasp her upper arms. She met his gaze without flinching, her lips parted slightly, her eyes tired and damp from tears.

"Marry me, Lovina. Marry me and we'll adopt Autumn as our very own. We can make a *familye* together, you and me. All you have to do is say yes," he said.

Her eyes widened and she stared at him like he'd just sprouted a second nose. She chewed her bottom lip and didn't say anything for several pounding moments.

"I'll admit I don't want to lose Autumn. But if I ever marry, it will be for love or not at all. And you don't love me, Jonah," she said.

Her voice sounded small and wounded. And oh, how he wanted to tell her what she so desperately wanted to hear. What they both needed was someone to love them. But she was right. He didn't love her.

Or did he?

Oh, he didn't know anymore. He cared for her. A great deal. He knew that without hesitation. But love? He thought he'd loved Fannie and look how that turned out. Now he realized he'd been more in love with the idea of marriage and having a *familye* of his own. He'd never really loved Fannie. Not for herself. In fact, the woman now grated on his nerves every time she was near. He wasn't a good judge of what love was. How could he ever know for sure that he loved Lovina? Really loved her, the way a man should love a woman. He didn't think he could know for sure.

So where did that leave them now? Here he sat with Lovina, and he couldn't say the words out loud to her. He wanted to but didn't dare. Because he would never lie to her.

She pulled free of his grasp. "Please, Jonah, no more talk. Just take me *heemet* now."

She faced forward, her lips and shoulders tight, her little chin hard as granite.

He took hold of the lead lines and did as she asked. When they pulled down the lane to his farm, the only sounds were the buggy wheels churning over the graveled driveway and the horse's low nicker of relief. Finally they were home. And yet neither of them belonged here. They were both alone in the world, and it appeared they always would be.

Lovina didn't wait for his aid. Without a word, she tossed aside the heavy quilts, threw open the buggy door and hopped out, dragging her medical bag with her. He sat there and watched as she disappeared inside the farmhouse. Soon *Dawdi* came out, his shoulders bent with fatigue as he limped on his cane toward the *dawdi haus*. The old man saw him and waved but kept on going. And still, Jonah sat there for some time, his heart just as frozen as the winter breeze blowing down from the mountains.

Chapter Twelve

The week before Christmas, Lovina sat at her kitchen table, filling out paperwork for her midwifery business. By law, she had ten days after baby Mary's birth to file her birth certificate with the state of Colorado. Lovina had met that deadline but needed to catch up on her bookkeeping. Each invoice for her services was handwritten and mailed or hand-delivered to her clients, who always paid in a timely fashion. It was painstaking work, but each envelope was a fulfilling reminder that she had a livelihood and could sustain herself.

A pot of ham-and-bean soup bubbled on the stove, filling the kitchen with a scrumptious aroma. Little Autumn sat in her bassinet on the table, wide-awake and kicking her legs like there was no tomorrow. It was late afternoon and she'd just had a bottle. With her tummy full, she was filled with energy and joy. Her little coos were a sweet distraction that Lovina couldn't resist and she set her pen down.

"You're happy today, aren't you, *liebchen*?" She rested her hand on the tiny girl's chest.

The baby smiled and chortled in response, completely melting Lovina's heart into a puddle.

She thought about the night not so long ago when Millie Troyer had given birth to little Mary. It had been a special time for all of them. Not only had Lovina participated in the miracle of birth but she'd received her first and only marriage proposal. She'd never forget the hurt in Jonah's eyes when she'd refused him. Oh, she'd been tempted, make no mistake about it. For just a moment, she'd allowed herself to believe he could love her the way she loved him. But then she'd shaken herself.

More than anything, she longed to experience the joys of being Jonah's wife and a mother to his children. But at what cost? She wouldn't accept his offer when he didn't love her. She'd had enough heartache in her life. Too much, in fact. She could never live in a loveless marriage. And Jonah couldn't love her. So she must leave. As soon as possible.

The rattle of a buggy drew her attention. Keeping an eye on the wriggling baby through the doorway, she stepped into the living room and peered out the window. Thin white candles surrounded by a green bed of pine boughs glimmered on the windowsill. It was the only Christmas decoration she ever put out. Not overly ostentatious but part of nature. Simple yet elegant. A reminder that Jesus Christ was the light of the world.

Bishop Yoder parked in front of the barn and stepped out to greet Jonah in the yard. It had rained heavily in the night, melting the remaining snow on the ground and leaving wide mud puddles along the lane. Frozen pools of ice lined the driveway, and she figured Jonah would be forced to break through the animal's water troughs so they could drink.

The two men turned her way, and she snapped back from the window. She didn't want to be caught spying on them. Through the filmy curtains, she saw them heading toward the house.

Her heart thudded. Maybe the bishop had some word about Autumn's mother. Maybe he'd come to take the girl away!

Hurrying to the kitchen, Lovina picked up

the baby and walked to the back door. She opened it wide as she greeted the two men.

"*Guder mariye*, bishop! *Komm* in. What brings you out to our place?" she asked.

Our place. She'd said the words before she thought better of it. Because this was Jonah's place. Not hers.

She tried to appear casual but inside, her heart was pounding and her mind was screaming. *No! Please don't take my baby from me. Not again.*

Both men doffed their black felt hats and wiped their damp boots on the rug. Lovina's gaze briefly locked with Jonah's. For a moment, she saw her fears mirrored in his eyes. Then he looked away.

"I've got some news for the two of you," Bishop Yoder said.

From his sober expression, she didn't think it was good. Lovina forced herself to remain calm.

Lifting one hand, she gestured toward the living room. "*Komm* in and sit down. Can I get you something to eat or drink?"

"*Ne*, I can't stay. I've been gone from my farm all day. I just wanted you and Jonah to know what has happened." He headed into the living room and plopped down on the sofa, holding his hat in one hand.

Jonah stood in front of the coffee table, his legs slightly spread in that commanding stance of his, as if he was self-assured and in control. He folded his hands behind his back and waited quietly. Though he appeared completely calm, an energy pulsed from him... an anxiousness she felt. And in his eyes, she saw a flicker of uncertainty.

"Yesterday, I received a letter from the bishop in Westcliffe," Bishop Yoder began.

Westcliffe was a neighboring town fifty miles away. Like Riverton, it had a population of around five thousand people with a small Amish community.

"His congregation has a teenage runaway girl who reportedly gave birth about three months ago. She's joined the *Englisch* world," he continued.

"Is she a minor?" Lovina asked.

"*Ne*, she is eighteen and a legal adult, though she was never baptized into our faith. Her name is Beth Gascho and her *mudder* died about a year ago. Beth had been living with her *vadder* and four elder brothers, but I'm afraid they've had a falling-out. It seems her *vadder* disapproves of her."

Lovina's hands tightened around Autumn. Even though the Amish believed in repentance and forgiveness, she'd been treated the same by her own father. People weren't always perfect and frequently hypocritical. Because of her own experience, she had instant compassion for Beth.

"Apparently Beth ran away a year ago during her *rumspringa* and took up with an *Englisch* boy," the bishop said.

Rumspringa, that rite of passage during adolescence when Amish teenagers experience freedom of choice without the rules of the *Ordnung* to hold them back.

"Beth's *vadder* didn't know until recently that his *dochder* had given birth out of wedlock. I've spoken to him and found him to be rather unforgiving. He wants nothing to do with Beth or her *boppli*," the bishop said.

The room suddenly whirled around Lovina. She reached to clasp the armrest of a chair and slid into the seat so she wouldn't fall over and drop Autumn.

"Lovina, are you *allrecht*?" Jonah was instantly by her side, leaning down to take the baby from her trembling hands. His look of concern only made matters worse.

"*Ja*, I'm fine." Her voice sounded hoarse as she averted her gaze from his caring face. But she wasn't fine. Not at all. It felt like she was reliving her own childhood trauma all over again, right alongside Beth.

"Beth is now living in Pueblo," the bishop said.

Pueblo was yet another neighboring town that was no more than sixty miles away but it had a much larger population of over one hundred thousand people. It would be easy for an Amish girl to get lost there.

"Wh-what is she doing in Pueblo? How is she living?" Lovina asked.

"She's waitressing at a restaurant and lives with another *Englisch* girl in a rather dowdy apartment," the bishop said. "Early this morning, I hired a driver to take me there. I first visited Beth's *vadder* and then I went and found her. I have only just returned from my journey."

The bishop had gone and met Beth!

"Do you think she is Autumn's *mudder*?" Jonah asked.

The bishop nodded. "I have no doubt. Before I revealed any information, she confirmed Autumn's name and birthdate and all the details of how you found the *boppli*. Beth wasn't happy I'd found her. She still has no idea where the *boppli*'s *vadder* is and believes he has left the state. Apparently she hasn't spoken with him in nine months, since she first told him she was expecting his child. I asked her to return here to Riverton with me and even offered a roof over her head until she can figure out how to support herself and her *boppli*."

"And what did she say?" Lovina prompted, her voice wobbly.

"She flatly refused."

The bishop's face looked severe. Lovina figured the encounter must have been highly unpleasant for him, especially since he'd offered to help the young woman.

"Beth insists she doesn't want to be a *mudder* or Amish anymore. But she did agree to one thing," he said.

"And what is that?" Jonah asked.

The bishop's gaze rested on Lovina like a leaden weight. "She has agreed to sign her parental rights over to Lovina in a formal adoption."

Lovina gasped. "Me! But why would she do that?"

Bishop Yoder lifted one shoulder. "It seems your reputation as a kind and caring midwife has filtered through the Amish community to Westcliffe. Beth thought by giving her *boppli* to you, she was providing Autumn with a *gut* home. I agree, except for one problem."

Lovina held perfectly still and waited. She didn't dare move. Didn't dare breathe.

"I will never agree to let Autumn remain with you permanently as long as you remain unmarried. The tenets of our faith dictate that a *boppli* deserves both a loving *vadder* and *mudder* to raise them. You are unmarried," he said.

A horrible, swelling silence followed. So loud that Lovina thought her ears might burst. She understood only too well. If she were *Englisch*, she could adopt Autumn and think nothing of it. But she was Amish and they lived by a different set of rules. And though she loved her faith and saw the benefit of raising a child with both parents, she couldn't help wishing her situation could be different. But she would never go against the doctrines of her faith.

Jonah opened his mouth and took a step forward but Lovina held out a hand, cutting him off. She knew what he was going to say. He would offer again to marry her. To sacrifice himself on the altar of matrimony in order to keep Autumn safe. But Lovina couldn't do that. Not even if it meant she could keep this precious baby girl as her own.

"I understand what it's like to give birth out of wedlock," she said. "I know how it feels to have a heartless *vadder* who won't help you. Perhaps if I spoke with Beth, I might be able to convince her to *komm* here. Once I move to my new *heemet*, she and Autumn can live with me."

The bishop leaned forward, his eyes filled with warmth as a kind smile tugged the corners of his mouth upward. "My dear, I thought you would offer that, so I posed the idea to Beth and still she refused. If she had agreed, I would let you do that. But I fear your generous efforts are wasted. You see, Beth was furious I'd found her. She has such an ugly spirit of resentment about her. She hates our faith and refuses to live it again. I don't want you to become the brunt of her anger. Not with your kind heart."

Oh, dear. That didn't sound good.

"At Beth's request, I paid a visit to Carl Nelson right before I came here to see you," Bishop Yoder said.

Jonah tilted his head to one side, his eyebrows pulled down in a quizzical frown. "You mean the attorney in town?"

The bishop nodded. "*Ja*, a few of our Amish people have used his legal services in the past. He is friendly to us Amish, and I believe he is trustworthy."

Lovina's mind swam with confusion. "But what does he have to do with Autumn?"

"I asked his legal advice, and he has agreed to help us with an adoption for Autumn," he said. "I know of a loving Amish couple whom I believe would cherish and raise her as their own. The *boppli* would want for nothing and would grow up Amish and learn to love the Lord."

Yes, that was what they all wanted for Autumn.

Looking down at her lap, Lovina folded her shaking hands. She swallowed hard, knowing she could not prevent the inevitable. The bishop would take the baby from them and give her to another *familye* to raise.

"It sounds like you've got everything worked out nice and tidy," Jonah said.

Lovina glanced up. Had she detected a trembly note of anguish in his voice? She wasn't sure because he turned away and dipped his face down to the baby before Lovina could see his expression. But she didn't need to. Just the fact that he was snuggling Autumn and holding her tight told Lovina all she needed to know. He didn't want to let go of this baby any more than she did.

"When the time comes, we know what to do," Bishop Yoder said. "But I need to make a few more inquiries first. I'm now working with the attorney to have Beth sign over her parental rights."

"But what about the *vadder*? What if the man returns and tries to take Autumn?" Jonah asked.

"Since Beth doesn't know how to find the man, Carl said the adoption must be published in the local newspaper," the bishop said. "It will take some patience but the attorney knows what to do legally. In the meantime, I would ask that you keep Autumn here a while longer, until I can put everything in order."

"Of course, as long as it takes," Lovina spoke without hesitation.

Anything to delay Autumn's departure. But Lovina knew it was a stay of execution. Eventually, the bishop would take the baby away.

The bishop stood. "*Gut*! I'll let you know as soon as everything is settled."

"But one more thing," Lovina said.

The two men looked at her with expectation.

"I… I'll be moving soon," she said. "Jonah is selling his farm, and I've been making inquiries for new living arrangements. I've found a small house in town that I can rent for a reasonable price and run my midwifery business from there."

The bishop frowned. So did Jonah.

"You found another place already?" Jonah said, his voice low and nervous.

"*Ja.* It needs heavy cleaning and a lot of paint but the rent is quite low," she said.

"I'm sorry to hear you're moving again," Bishop Yoder said. "I knew Jonah was planning to sell but hoped the present situation might have changed his mind."

The bishop looked at Jonah as he spoke. Jonah didn't say a word, and a heavy silence filled the room. The older man's gray eyes seemed to pierce a hole right through Jonah's head. But it made no difference. Not for Lovina. Jonah could take his farm off the market and stay here forever, but she must go. The sooner, the better. Because she loved him. Heaven help her, she truly loved him beyond anything she could comprehend. And staying here would only bring her more pain. Living so near to him. Seeing him every day. Working with him. She couldn't do it anymore.

"But there is still time. Perhaps you'll both change your minds," the bishop said as he walked to the front door and left without another word.

Lovina didn't think so.

She stared out the living room window, waiting until his buggy pulled away from the farm. She longed to call him back. To tell him she would accept Jonah's offer just so they could keep Autumn. But she couldn't do that. And nothing would change her mind.

"Lovina, I know you're upset," Jonah said.

He stood beside her in the living room as they both stared out the wide picture window and watched the bishop's buggy fade from view. Although Jonah had expected this news, it wasn't what he'd wanted to hear. He was still holding Autumn. As if sensing the morose mood in the room, the baby began to fuss and wriggle in his arms.

Lovina turned and took the baby from him, then walked into the kitchen, where she retrieved a bottle for the little girl. Jonah followed, his ears echoing with all the things the bishop had told them. There was so much Jonah longed to say to Lovina but he didn't dare. She'd only reject him again.

"It's all settled," Lovina said. "Soon, the bishop will return to take Autumn to her new *familye*. There will be a formal adoption, which will make things nice and legal. We don't want Beth or the *Englisch vadder* to show up years later and try to take Autumn after she's bonded with her new *familye*."

"*Ne*, we don't want that," he said.

"And I'll be moving soon. You'll sell your farm and go back east. Everyone can return to the lives they've chosen."

Jonah blinked, her words striking him as hard as a fist to the gut. But she was right. How they lived was a choice they each made. They could choose the path they wanted to take. And right now, he didn't want to lose Autumn. He didn't want to lose Lovina, either.

She sniffed and he realized she was crying. Standing at the stove, she had her back to him. The baby had become very quiet, peering over Lovina's shoulder at him with her big blue eyes. It was as if she were telling him to do something about this. Right now!

Letting his heart guide him, Jonah stepped over to Lovina. He gripped her arms gently and turned her around. She hung her head, staring at the floor as she wiped her eyes. The baby waved her arms and grabbed a handful of Jonah's hair, pulling him closer. He placed one finger beneath Lovina's chin and lifted her face so she was forced to meet his gaze. Her eyes swam with tears and were filled with so much hurt and betrayal that all he wanted was to see her smile again.

"Please don't cry, Lovina. It's all going to be okay," he whispered, drawing nearer.

Before he realized what was happening, he kissed her. Or she kissed him. He wasn't sure which. He only knew how it made him feel. Happy, wild and free. The kiss was so gentle, like a soft caress. And for that moment in time, emotion overwhelmed Jonah. Surely there was no better place on earth than right here in his kitchen. Lovina's kitchen. Their home. This was where he wanted to be.

Wasn't it?

Lovina exhaled a little sigh and he felt her warm breath against his face. The baby rested her hand against his cheek, as if showing her approval. For several profound moments, the three of them stood there in a close huddle. Then Lovina drew her face away, and he realized he had enfolded her and the baby in his arms.

"Jonah, don't." Lovina pressed one hand against his chest, pushing him away.

He stepped back, his mind scattering. What had he done?

"Marry me, Lovina. We will do well together. It's the only way," he whispered low.

"*Ne*, I will not," she said.

She moved over to the fridge, as if she were desperate to put some distance between them. Autumn immediately began to cry.

Jonah's gaze followed them as Lovina prepared a bottle for the baby.

"I care for you. I do," he said.

Lovina stared at him, her eyes filled with outrage. "You care for me?"

He nodded, his mouth dry as chalk. "I do. Very much."

She snorted. "*Ach*, we each care for lots of people, Jonah. That doesn't mean we want to marry them. Marriage is for keeps. It means living together, sharing the *gut* and the bad forever. Caring isn't enough. Not for me."

She turned her back on him. As usual, he'd said the wrong thing at the wrong time. But how could he make her understand? They had to be together. They must!

"You know our church elders will never agree to let you keep Autumn without us being wed. The bishop made that clear today," he said.

"I will not marry you and that's final," she said. She turned and met his gaze, a somber, resolute expression on her face. "Instead, why don't you sell the farm to me?"

He tilted his head to one side, thinking he must have heard her wrong. "What?"

"You want to leave and I need a place to live. I have a little money saved and a *gut* income from my business. What is your asking price? Perhaps I can qualify for a loan and buy the place," she said, her voice firm.

His mouth dropped open in surprise. She wanted to buy his farm? She must be teasing. But as he stared at her unwavering expression, he realized she was dead serious.

As if through a fog, he named his price. The very amount he'd given to the real estate agent in town. It wasn't high. Just enough to pay off what he owed and move him and *Dawdi* back east where they could start anew.

Lovina frowned and reached for the bottle, giving it to the baby. Autumn latched on and sucked furiously, as though she didn't like this conversation any more than Jonah did.

"I'm afraid I can't afford that much. Would you be willing to sell me just the farmhouse?" Lovina asked without looking at him.

He leaned against the wall and looped his thumbs through his suspenders. "*Ne*, I'm afraid the house would have to go with the farm. Otherwise, I would never be able to sell the acreage. And without a house, *Dawdi* and I would have no place to live if we can't sell and are forced to stay and work the land."

Her shoulders sagged in resignation. It seemed they were at a deadlock.

"Then I will move to town as I planned. I… I have things to do. If you don't mind, I need to get back to work," she said.

Okay, he could take a hint. She was bluntly inviting him to leave.

Nodding, he turned toward the door. He rested his hand on the knob, his mind churning with what he should say. But nothing came to mind. His hand trembled. He couldn't leave but he couldn't stay.

As he stepped outside, a blast of frigid wind struck him in the face. He knew what was at stake. Soon, Autumn would be taken away. Lovina would go live somewhere else. Jonah would eventually sell his farm and move back east with *Dawdi*. They would never see each other again and that thought crushed Jonah's heart like nothing he'd experienced before. Now that he was really faced with losing Lovina for good, a flash of insight speared his icy heart. With perfect clarity, he realized how deeply he loved her and he knew he couldn't let this happen.

Finally. Finally, he understood what his own mother must have felt when she'd abandoned him years earlier. The fear and uncertainty must have caused her to run away and seek another life. Anger, hurt, shame and dissatisfaction with herself must have caused her to run. She'd made some bad choices but was too young and inexperienced to see how to make it right. And knowing this, Jonah was finally able to let go of his anger at her. Now that he understood her motives, he could forgive her.

But now he had a new dilemma.

How could he convince Lovina that he loved her and wanted to be with her forever? If he told her now, she would laugh in his face. She would think he was saying what she wanted to hear just so they could keep Autumn. It was too late to make this right between them. Or was it?

Chapter Thirteen

The very next day, Jonah drove one of his big Percheron draft horses into his spacious driveway and headed for the barn. Though it was bitter cold outside, he'd taken advantage of the clear weather to clean out the stalls and haul the manure out to his fields. The ground was frozen but he'd spread the fertilizer across the barren land, knowing it would benefit the summer crops.

Stepping to the back of the horse, he unhitched the wagon. The afternoon sun glinted off the metal roof of the shed, and he lifted an arm to shield his eyes as he glanced at the farmhouse. Christmas was just a few days away, yet his heart felt heavy as he considered paying a visit to Lovina. He'd made a final decision that would impact his life forever and had gone into town earlier that morning.

There was no going back. Now they needed to talk.

Gripping the halter on the Percheron, he led the gentle giant into the barn. He'd tossed the animal some hay and rubbed him down when *Dawdi* burst into the stall.

"Jonah! I'm so glad you're back."

He turned as *Dawdi* hobbled toward him on his cane. The old man was dressed in his warm winter coat and black boots. He sounded breathless and anxious, his bushy eyebrows drawn together in an urgent frown.

"What is it? What's wrong?" Jonah asked.

"It's Lovina. Just after lunch, she packed a bunch of boxes into her buggy and drove into town. She took Autumn with her. She's gone," *Dawdi* said.

Boxes! Was she moving already? She'd told the bishop she'd be leaving soon but Jonah thought he had more time. But no. She'd left!

A flash of panic blazed through his chest. He'd spent the last twenty hours trying to figure out how to convince her that he loved her and wanted to marry her. But now he was out of time. She was gone!

"Here!" Jonah handed a small bucket of oats to his grandfather, knowing the older man would feed it to the Percheron.

Scrambling out of the stall, Jonah hurried

over to his road horse, Bob. Without a glance at his grandfather, he tossed a blanket and then an old dusty saddle onto the animal's back.

"I've got to go after her. Can you take care of things here for a while?" he asked.

Standing nearby, *Dawdi* took hold of the halter to steady the horse. "Of course. I've got this. You go bring them *heemet*. And don't take *ne* for an answer this time."

Jonah had told his grandfather how Lovina had refused his proposal. He paused a moment as he looked at the older man. *Dawdi* nodded and smiled. It was the only reassurance Jonah needed.

In a single bound, he swung up onto Bob's back and kicked his heels. The Amish rarely rode horses. The animal wasn't used to this and danced around nervously for several seconds, then sprang out the barn doors like a racehorse breaking from the starting gate.

As he sped away, Jonah leaned low over Bob's neck and held on tight. Needles of cold lashed his face but he barely felt it. One thought pounded his brain. He had to find Lovina. He had to see her, speak to her and convince her he loved her. He must bring her back home. Now that he was faced with losing her for good, everything became so clear in his heart and mind. He loved her. More than anything else on earth. He couldn't lose her or Autumn. Not now, when he'd finally realized what they meant to him. His future happiness depended on his success.

For several minutes, he clung to the horse, with only the sounds of the winter breeze and thudding hooves striking the road. Finally, he saw the outskirts of town. Only then did he realize he had no idea where to go. Lovina hadn't told him where she was moving. But surely it wouldn't be difficult to find an Amish buggy in this small town. He'd scour every street searching for her. And if that failed, he'd pay an urgent visit to the real estate agent. Jonah would beg for her address. He'd find her. Whatever it took…

There she was! Parked on the main street, right in front of the general store. She stood beside her buggy, reaching inside to lift a heavy box out of the back. She set it on the boardwalk.

He pulled Bob to a skidding stop. As he jumped out of the saddle, Lovina whirled around in surprise.

"Jonah! What are you doing here?" she cried, her eyes wide, her cheeks flushed.

"Lovina, I had to find you," he said, looping the reins around a post that supported the covered portico overhead.

"Why? What's happened?"

He scanned the area, then peered inside the buggy. "Where's Autumn?"

Lovina jerked a thumb toward the store. "She's inside with Mrs. Maupin. Why?"

Berta Maupin owned the grocery store. She was a kind, elderly woman who'd always treated the Amish well.

"*Gut*! We need to talk," he said.

Lovina snorted. "*Ne*! The time for talking is over. I've got work to do."

As she reached to take another box out of the buggy, Jonah stepped in front of her, impeding her progress.

She sighed. "Jonah, please..."

"I love you, Lovina. I do!"

"Don't say things you don't mean."

"I do mean it. With every beat of my heart. When I got *heemet* and *Dawdi* told me you'd left, I... I couldn't stand to lose you. I raced after you. I've got to bring you back, Lovina. Please, listen to me," he said.

She stared at him with disbelief. A car zipped past on the street and their horses shifted restlessly.

Lovina shook her head. "It's not going to

work and we both know it. You're selling your farm."

He saw the hurt in her eyes as she turned away.

"I'm not selling the farm."

She whirled around. "What do you mean?"

"I rode into town first thing this morning and visited my real estate agent. I took my farm off the market. I'm not selling it after all. I'm staying right here, in Riverton."

She blinked those beautiful blue eyes at him, her lips parted slightly. "You're not selling? You're staying?"

He nodded, letting it sink in. Then he reached out and pulled her toward him. He expected her to jerk free but she didn't fight him. Not one bit.

"But why? I… I thought you wanted to leave?" she said, her voice a breathy whisper.

"That was before I fell in love with you," he said. "I spent a restless night trying to figure out how to convince you that I love you and want to make a *familye* with you for real. And I realized it might take me a long time, but I'd do whatever it took to make you trust me."

Her eyes narrowed suspiciously. "You couldn't change your mind that fast. Why should I believe you?"

"Because it's true. When *Dawdi* told me

you were moving today, I was panic-stricken with the thought of never seeing you again. I can't lose you, Lovina. I love you."

She took a step closer. "But I'm not moving today."

He squinted in confusion and gestured toward the boxes. "Then what's all this?"

She gave a low laugh, the sound soft and sweet to his ears. "It's the annual food drive. For a month now, the women in our *Gmay* have been bringing canned goods to me. Most of them pay regular visits anyway for their *boppli* needs, so I was assigned to bring it all into town. Mrs. Maupin is the chair of the food drive and will see that it gets delivered to people in need throughout the community."

Ah, now he understood all the boxes. She wasn't moving after all. At least not today.

Before he could stop it from happening, a smile of relief spread across his face. Though the Amish took care of one another, they also frequently participated in works of service with their *Englisch* neighbors. Lovina wasn't moving. Yet. But that could soon change. Unless he convinced her otherwise.

"I can't tell you how happy that makes me," he said.

She heaved a disgruntled sigh. "I don't understand, Jonah. Sometimes you make me so crazy."

He laughed. He couldn't help himself. Because she made him crazy. Crazy in love.

"I've been confused, too. But right now, I've never been filled with more clarity. I know we both could go on and live our lives without romantic entanglements. We'd have a perfectly safe and very lonely existence, Lovina. But we'd also never know the joy of love we could have together. And that isn't what *Gott* wants for us. I don't want to go through life without you. I can only hope and pray that, one day, you can love me as much as I love you. Please say you'll marry me and make me the happiest man in the world."

As he waited for her answer, his breath was shallow in his chest. He couldn't say another word. He'd done what he'd vowed he would never do again and laid his heart bare, giving her the power to shatter it into a thousand tiny pieces once more. Now it was in her hands.

Lovina stood in front of Jonah, gazing at his earnest face. She couldn't believe what he said. After all they'd been through, how could she trust him now? He loved her? Unthinkable. Something she'd only dreamed of. And yet he'd said it several times.

"*Ach*, Jonah! Your timing is terrible. But in my heart, I so want to believe you," she said.

Oh, dear. Maybe she shouldn't have said that. But if he really meant what he said and could gather the courage to say it out loud, then so could she.

He stepped closer, the tips of his scuffed boots touching the toes of her clean, practical shoes. She gazed up into his smiling face, lost in the translucent depths of his eyes.

"Believe me, Lovina. You know I wouldn't say it if it wasn't true."

Oh, she couldn't fight him anymore. Not now when he was saying what she'd wanted to hear for so long.

"Oh, Jonah!"

He took her hands into his and she didn't resist. Their noses touched and she thought he might kiss her. She even hungered for it.

"Ahum!"

Someone cleared their throat behind her and she snapped back.

"Bishop Yoder!" she exclaimed.

Yes, the bishop stood right beside her on the boardwalk. The heat of mortification burned her cheeks. She had no idea how much of their conversation he'd overheard. Out here on the open street, for all the world to see. What must he think of them?

"Wh-what are you doing here?" she asked before she could stop herself. She didn't want to sound rude. Not to this kind man.

"I was looking for you two," he said.

Bundled in his warm winter attire, he smiled broadly. "I was just out at your farm, and Noah told me you were here."

Lovina stepped away from Jonah but he didn't release her hand. And that touched her heart like nothing else could. It was a blatant, physical declaration that she belonged to him. That they were a couple and he wanted everyone to know.

"What did you want to see us about?" Jonah asked.

The bishop stepped down into the street, standing close. "I overheard Jonah's proposal and I feel I must intercede. I have news for both of you. It seems the elderly *Englisch* farmer who owns the land bordering Jonah's property died two days ago."

"He did?" Jonah said.

"*Ja*, and his *kinder* don't want his farm. Instead, they want to sell it off as soon as possible. It would give Jonah thirty more acres of land, which is plenty to make his farm prosper."

Jonah's mouth dropped open, and he gaped at the bishop. A zing of happiness ripped through Lovina's heart. She knew this was what he wanted. And it looked like he would get it.

"That's great news!" Jonah said.

"*Gut*! Because I told them you wanted the property. Our *Gmay* will ensure you have the funds to buy it immediately," Bishop Yoder said.

"I have some money saved and would love to invest it in our farm. Together, we can afford to buy the extra land," Lovina said.

Jonah blinked at her. "Our farm? Together? You mean...you'll marry me?"

She smiled, her heart overflowing with joy. "How can I not when you're the love of my life?"

"Oh, Lovina. That's more than I ever dared hope for. Now it will truly be our *heemet*."

"*Ja*, it will." She gazed at him with elation.

The bishop chuckled. "There's just one more thing you two ought to know. That couple I've had in mind to adopt little Autumn..."

"*Ja?*" Jonah urged.

"It's you two," the bishop said. "I always knew you'd come around eventually, though you took your sweet time realizing how much you love each other. But I'm glad to hear you've finally arrived at the decision to wed." He looked between the two of them. "You are getting married, right?"

Jonah gazed adoringly into Lovina's eyes… the way so many of her expectant fathers looked at their wives. Lovina searched Jonah's face for any doubts, any reservations at all, but saw nothing but hope and love.

"You will marry me, won't you, Lovina?" he asked softly, enticingly.

She nodded her head, no longer willing to fight against the feelings in her heart. "*Ach*, of course I will. Because you see, Jonah, I love you, too. So very much!"

With a loud whoop, Jonah pulled her into his arms and whirled her around until she was dizzy. He kissed her right there on Main Street, in front of the bishop and anyone who chose to look. And when he finally set her on her feet, they all laughed.

The bishop cleared his throat. "Um, I think I'd better go now. I'll talk with you again on Christmas Day and you can be married soon after. But I believe Autumn has found her permanent *familye*. She belongs with the two of you. I'm glad to say I won't have to search for another *familye* to take her after all."

He turned and walked away, the heels of his boots thudding against the planks of the boardwalk lining the street. Watching him go,

Lovina couldn't believe their good fortune. It had come so unexpectedly. So magnificently. Love and *familye*. The best Christmas gifts of all.

"As the bishop suggested, I'd like to get married right after Christmas," Jonah said.

His arm was still firmly around her back, holding her tight against his side. She nodded, feeling suddenly shy with this newfound closeness between them.

"*Ja*, I'll marry you. Just as soon as we can."

He kissed her once more, then let her go and turned toward the buggy. "*Gut*! I'm going to get the rest of these boxes out and then we're going to retrieve our *boppli* from Mrs. Maupin and go *heemet*. We have a lot of plans to make."

Lovina smiled, more than pleased by his words. After all, she'd just gotten the desire of her heart. A loving husband and sweet baby daughter. What more could she ask for?

Epilogue

※

One year later

Lovina stepped out of the county courthouse in Cañon City, Colorado, and glanced up at the gray sky. Another snowstorm was coming in tonight but she had no doubt they'd be safely home before then.

Tugging the warm blankets tightly around Autumn, she noticed someone had spread pellets of ice melt across the slick sidewalk. She was extra careful as she carried the little girl toward the parking lot. Autumn was over a year old now and toddling all around the place, getting into everything. But Lovina didn't mind one bit.

It was the week before Christmas and they had so much to celebrate. It seemed the year had flown by. So much had happened in the past twelve months that she could hardly contain her excitement.

An *Englisch* driver waited for them in his parked car. Lovina held back, giving Jonah time to join her. She didn't have long to wait. He emerged from the tall double doors, accompanied by *Dawdi* Noah, Bishop Yoder and Carl Nelson, their attorney from Riverton. Lovina watched as the four men talked together for several minutes. She didn't mind, knowing they were finalizing the adoption. She cherished the few moments she had alone with Autumn.

The baby held out a chubby hand and waved at the drifting snowflakes that were starting to fall. Lovina smiled and snuggled the girl close.

"You like snow, don't you, *liebchen*?" Lovina said.

Autumn babbled incoherently in response, her sweet voice filling Lovina's heart with so much happiness that she thought it might burst. The baby looked so cute, bundled in her warm blankets and wearing the miniature white organdy prayer *kapp* Lovina had made especially for this occasion.

"*Ach*, how are my two *maed* doing?"

Lovina turned as Jonah slid an arm behind her back and pulled her in close. Upon seeing her daddy, Autumn gave a gleeful laugh and clapped her little hands.

"*Dat,*" she cried.

He smiled wide. "*Ja*, Itty-Bit, I'm your *daed.*"

After assuring herself no one was watching, Lovina snuggled against him. Though the Amish rarely showed open displays of affection, this was a special day and she couldn't resist his charm.

"We're *gut*, and I'm glad to have all this legal stuff behind us. All I want to do is glory in this *wundervoll* day," Lovina said.

He leaned close, brushing the baby's face with a gentle caress before he kissed Lovina's brow. "*Ja*, we have much to celebrate. I thought we could enjoy lunch at the restaurant down the street before we go *heemet.*"

A pleasant fissure of surprise pulsed over Lovina. They rarely ate out. Leave it to Jonah to make this day even more memorable.

"I thought we might like to walk together and have a few moments to ourselves. Ted is taking *Dawdi*, Bishop Yoder and Carl in the car and we'll meet them over there."

Ted Calhoun was their *Englisch* driver. Since Cañon City was fifteen miles from Riverton, it was too far to drive by buggy.

Ted frequently drove the Amish in those situations.

"We'll have a real celebration with all of us there," Lovina said.

She glanced at the parking lot and noticed Ted had pulled his blue sedan into afternoon traffic. *Dawdi* sat in the back seat, waving to them. Lovina lifted Autumn's hand and waved back.

"Say bye-bye," she coaxed the girl.

"Bye-bye," Autumn mimicked in a tiny voice.

They laughed, delighted by their sweet little daughter.

"*Allrecht.* Let's go." Jonah took the baby from Lovina, and she held tight to his solid arm as they headed down the street.

"Isn't it a beautiful day?" Lovina breathed a sigh of relief, grateful the adoption was finalized.

Over the past months, there had been moments when she'd wondered if Autumn would ever really belong to them. But Beth Gascho had been as good as her word and signed over her parental rights. Finally, Autumn was legally and lawfully their child. No one could take her away. They were truly a *familye* now. The best Christmas gift Lovina could ever hope for.

"Lovely, indeed," Jonah said, gazing at her.

Lovina knew he wasn't talking about the day. She smiled, feeling suddenly out of sorts. Jonah had a way of making her feel so special. Like she meant everything to him. And she loved him for it.

They walked for several moments in silence, each of them lost in the thrill of the day. Then…

"Lovina, you don't have any regrets about marrying me, do you?" Jonah asked.

She glanced at him. They'd been married ten months now but even she could hardly believe how blessed they were.

"*Ne*, not ever! The Lord has been so *gut* to us. I never thought I could be so happy," she said, speaking the truth.

"How about you? Do you have any regrets?" she asked.

"Just one. I wish I'd asked you sooner. I was a dolt for taking so long," he confessed.

They both laughed.

"Not a dolt. Just a man who needed to figure out what he really wanted," she said.

"And I want you." He was looking at her again, so intently her face flushed.

"It was soon enough. But I'm afraid we'll have to make room for more. I may need a midwife of my own," she said.

He frowned and threw her a quizzical look. "What do you mean?"

She slowed and finally came to a halt on the sidewalk. When she rested her free hand across her abdomen, she looked up and hoped he caught her meaning. She delivered babies but it wasn't the Amish way to speak openly of pregnancy. Especially not out on the street like this.

"Lovina!" he whispered. "Am I going to be a father again?"

She nodded, speaking low so no one would overhear. "In the summer."

He released a pent-up laugh and hugged her tight. "That's *wundervoll* news! Maybe we'll have a little *bu* this time. *Ach*, how I adore you."

"And I love you," she whispered.

"*Lub* you," Autumn echoed their words.

They stared at their daughter, then burst into laughter. She was starting to say more words every day but these were the best of all.

As they continued on their way, they discussed their farm, the extra crops Jonah would plant in the spring, their EMT and midwifery work, and possible names for their new baby. Their life was so full and busy. Lovina loved listening to Jonah talk. Like her, he was happy and animated today. She breathed a contented sigh and enjoyed their walk together. Her heart was so full as she looked toward the future with her husband, and she couldn't ask *Gott* for anything more.

* * * * *

Dear Reader,

Have you ever been judgmental of someone else? And after judging them, did you discover that you were wrong or had based your judgments on half the facts? Or maybe you came to the realization that you had as many faults as the person you were being critical of. I think, sooner or later, all of us will experience this dilemma. That's what this story is about. Learning not to judge others. Because we all are sinners. And we never know what repentance process someone else has already gone through. Maybe they have been forgiven, so where does that leave us? By judging them, we have now become the sinner.

Life is never easy, but the atonement of Jesus Christ offers each of us the opportunity to repent and be forgiven. When we follow the Savior's example, we can receive His healing balm for our own hearts as well as help others do the same. But the atonement isn't just for you or me. It's for all of God's children. Every single one. And we must exercise faith, repentance and forgiveness in order to truly "follow Him."

I hope you enjoyed reading this story and I invite you to visit my website at www.LeighBale.com to learn more about my books.

May you find peace in the Lord's words!
Leigh Bale

Get 4 FREE REWARDS!

We'll send you 2 FREE Books plus 2 FREE Mystery Gifts.

Love Inspired books feature uplifting stories where faith helps guide you through life's challenges and discover the promise of a new beginning.

FREE Value Over $20

YES! Please send me 2 FREE Love Inspired Romance novels and my 2 FREE mystery gifts (gifts are worth about $10 retail). After receiving them, if I don't wish to receive any more books, I can return the shipping statement marked "cancel." If I don't cancel, I will receive 6 brand-new novels every month and be billed just $5.24 each for the regular-print edition or $5.99 each for the larger-print edition in the U.S., or $5.74 each for the regular-print edition or $6.24 each for the larger-print edition in Canada. That's a savings of at least 13% off the cover price. It's quite a bargain! Shipping and handling is just 50¢ per book in the U.S. and $1.25 per book in Canada.* I understand that accepting the 2 free books and gifts places me under no obligation to buy anything. I can always return a shipment and cancel at any time. The free books and gifts are mine to keep no matter what I decide.

Choose one:
☐ **Love Inspired Romance Regular-Print**
(105/305 IDN GNWC)

☐ **Love Inspired Romance Larger-Print**
(122/322 IDN GNWC)

Name (please print)

Address   Apt. #

City   State/Province   Zip/Postal Code

Email: Please check this box ☐ if you would like to receive newsletters and promotional emails from Harlequin Enterprises ULC and its affiliates. You can unsubscribe anytime.

Mail to the Harlequin Reader Service:
IN U.S.A.: P.O. Box 1341, Buffalo, NY 14240-8531
IN CANADA: P.O. Box 603, Fort Erie, Ontario L2A 5X3

Want to try 2 free books from another series? Call 1-800-873-8635 or visit www.ReaderService.com.

*Terms and prices subject to change without notice. Prices do not include sales taxes, which will be charged (if applicable) based on your state or country of residence. Canadian residents will be charged applicable taxes. Offer not valid in Quebec. This offer is limited to one order per household. Books received may not be as shown. Not valid for current subscribers to Love Inspired Romance books. All orders subject to approval. Credit or debit balances in a customer's account(s) may be offset by any other outstanding balance owed by or to the customer. Please allow 4 to 6 weeks for delivery. Offer available while quantities last.

Your Privacy—Your information is being collected by Harlequin Enterprises ULC, operating as Harlequin Reader Service. For a complete summary of the information we collect, how we use this information and to whom it is disclosed, please visit our privacy notice located at corporate.harlequin.com/privacy-notice. From time to time we may also exchange your personal information with reputable third parties. If you wish to opt out of this sharing of your personal information, please visit readerservice.com/consumerchoice or call 1-800-873-8635. **Notice to California Residents**—Under California law, you have specific rights to control and access your data. For more information on these rights and how to exercise them, visit corporate.harlequin.com/california-privacy.

LIR21R2

Get 4 FREE REWARDS!

We'll send you 2 FREE Books plus 2 FREE Mystery Gifts.

Harlequin Heartwarming Larger-Print books will connect you to uplifting stories where the bonds of friendship, family and community unite.

FREE Value Over $20

YES! Please send me 2 FREE Harlequin Heartwarming Larger-Print novels and my 2 FREE mystery gifts (gifts worth about $10 retail). After receiving them, if I don't wish to receive any more books, I can return the shipping statement marked "cancel." If I don't cancel, I will receive 4 brand-new larger-print novels every month and be billed just $5.74 per book in the U.S. or $6.24 per book in Canada. That's a savings of at least 21% off the cover price. It's quite a bargain! Shipping and handling is just 50¢ per book in the U.S. and $1.25 per book in Canada.* I understand that accepting the 2 free books and gifts places me under no obligation to buy anything. I can always return a shipment and cancel at any time. The free books and gifts are mine to keep no matter what I decide.

161/361 HDN GNPZ

Name (please print)

Address   Apt. #

City   State/Province   Zip/Postal Code

Email: Please check this box ☐ if you would like to receive newsletters and promotional emails from Harlequin Enterprises ULC and its affiliates. You can unsubscribe anytime.

Mail to the Harlequin Reader Service:
IN U.S.A.: P.O. Box 1341, Buffalo, NY 14240-8531
IN CANADA: P.O. Box 603, Fort Erie, Ontario L2A 5X3

Want to try 2 free books from another series? Call 1-800-873-8635 or visit www.ReaderService.com.

---

*Terms and prices subject to change without notice. Prices do not include sales taxes, which will be charged (if applicable) based on your state or country of residence. Canadian residents will be charged applicable taxes. Offer not valid in Quebec. This offer is limited to one order per household. Books received may not be as shown. Not valid for current subscribers to Harlequin Heartwarming Larger-Print books. All orders subject to approval. Credit or debit balances in a customer's account(s) may be offset by any other outstanding balance owed by or to the customer. Please allow 4 to 6 weeks for delivery. Offer available while quantities last.

Your Privacy—Your information is being collected by Harlequin Enterprises ULC, operating as Harlequin Reader Service. For a complete summary of the information we collect, how we use this information and to whom it is disclosed, please visit our privacy notice located at corporate.harlequin.com/privacy-notice. From time to time we may also exchange your personal information with reputable third parties. If you wish to opt out of this sharing of your personal information, please visit readerservice.com/consumerschoice or call 1-800-873-8635. **Notice to California Residents**—Under California law, you have specific rights to control and access your data. For more information on these rights and how to exercise them, visit corporate.harlequin.com/california-privacy.

HW21R2

COMING NEXT MONTH FROM
Love Inspired

NURSING HER AMISH NEIGHBOR
Brides of Lost Creek • by Marta Perry
Seeking a break from her nursing duties, Miriam Stoltzfus returns to Lost Creek only to be met with her most difficult patient yet—her childhood neighbor, Matthew King. While he's crushed in spirit after being injured in the accident that killed his brother, can she heal his physical wounds *and* his heart?

BLENDED AMISH BLESSINGS
Redemption's Amish Legacies • by Patricia Johns
When widower Paul Ebersole's kitten causes havoc in Haddie Petersheim's creamery, they agree to repair the store together. Soon they realize they have much in common. Supporting each other with their families might bring them closer than they ever imagined...

THEIR UNBREAKABLE BOND
Rocky Mountain Family • by Deb Kastner
Training avalanche rescue dogs in Colorado was never in Stone Keller's plans—especially with Felicity Winslow, his best friend's sister. But after a reckless motorcycle accident ruins his rodeo career, Felicity and the dogs could be just what he needs to put the pieces of his life back together...

A COWBOY TO RELY ON
Wyoming Ranchers • by Jill Kemerer
Still processing his grief, Jet Mayer is shocked to learn his late brother had a secret wife and child. Caring for his sister-in-law, Holly Mayer, and infant niece is a responsibility Jet's not sure he can handle. But could opening his home to them be exactly what they all need?

SEARCHING FOR HOME
by Jill Weatherholt
Heading home to recover from an injury, bull rider Luke Beckett plans to keep to himself—until he comes face-to-face with his ex-girlfriend, physical therapist Meg Brennan, and the triplets in her care. With Meg's troubled little nephew reminding Luke of himself, helping out this makeshift family might be just what the doctor ordered...

HIS ROAD TO REDEMPTION
by Lisa Jordan
Battle-scarred veteran Micah Holland is trying to turn his life around. When he inherits a farm, he discovers his co-owner is childhood frenemy Paige Watson. Paige has her own plans for the place, which don't include him. Can they set aside their differences and create a lasting legacy?

LOOK FOR THESE AND OTHER LOVE INSPIRED BOOKS WHEREVER BOOKS ARE SOLD, INCLUDING MOST BOOKSTORES, SUPERMARKETS, DISCOUNT STORES AND DRUGSTORES.

LICNM1221